THE
DIAMOND
SMUGGLERS

by
O. M. BROOKES

This story is for my son and my daughter, and also for those other children, both Maori and pakeha, who taught me so much over the years when I thought I was teaching them...

CONTENTS

The setting of the story is Napier and Wellington, New Zealand, but the characters are fictitious.

PROLOGUE

THE MAN IN the fur-collared overcoat paused as he hastened up the gangway, slipped a hand into his pocket, and glanced quickly and furtively over his shoulder. His footsteps sounded dully in the cold morning.

"Ah, there you are!" The captain slapped him heartily on the back as he at last stood on the deck. "Meet Mr. Bulke, our new purser. Very useful man, too."

The stranger smiled briefly, and silently waited for the new purser to go.

"Staying long in Rotterdam?" he grunted when he and the captain were alone. "I've to return to Amsterdam to-night."

"To-night? You have the—assignment?" The captain mopped his bald head in a sudden wave of anxiety.

"Yes. Yes. You go to—?"

"London, and then Napier, New Zealand."

The stranger nodded, satisfied.

Again he peered furtively over his shoulder. His hand came out of his pocket, and lingered near a coil of rope.

"Well, see you next time!" The captain again slapped him heartily on the back.

"Good luck to—!" the man's sentence was cut off short as he noticed the purser approaching.

The stranger's steps slowed when he left the ship. Deliberately he turned and gazed at her. He gazed for a long moment until his eyes rested on her bows, and the name painted there—*Golden Star.*

CHAPTER ONE

ALONG THE RUNWAY

OVER NAPIER airport the aeroplane from Auckland turned, slid lower and lower, and glided smoothly on to the runway, taxying to a quiet standstill. The mobile steps were pushed into place, the door of the gleaming aircraft opened, and out filed the passengers. At the end came Uncle Bob, dressed in his best blue-grey suit. He was followed closely by tall, thirteen-year-old Lan.

Uncle Bob pushed back his panama hat, as they paused in the sunshine, looking for Aunt Jenny.

"There she is! There's Aunt Jenny!" Uncle Bob strode towards her.

Lan looked at his aunt eagerly, and saw the laughter lines that crinkled at the corners of her blue eyes.

Aunt Jenny hid her surprise. Why, Alan was almost a man, tall and thin and dark-haired like all the Sherwoods. But those grey eyes were his mother's.

"Alan!" Aunt Jenny cried, hugging Lan joyfully.

"Hello, Aunt Jenny." Lan's English accent sounded short and crisp to New Zealand ears. "It's strange to be in New Zealand at last."

His eyes ran down his new clothes. He still felt strange in the cotton T-shirt, the drill shorts, the sandals without socks, and the sunhat with the flap to protect his neck. His skin looked pale, compared with the golden-brown appearance of Uncle Bob and Aunt Jenny.

"Uncle brought grand clothes for me to change into when he met me in Auckland. I don't think I'd have lasted long in thick London ones," Lan turned to his aunt.

"You wouldn't," Aunt Jenny agreed briskly. "But I'd no idea you were so tall, Alan. You'll be out of them in no time." She led them to an old, weary-looking car.

"Here's the old bomb. It's not ours. A chap at the Customs office, where I work, lent it to me while our car is having a re-bore," Uncle Bob explained in his deep voice, while his bushy, brown eyebrows descended and moved together to form a thick smudge.

"What about the luggage?" Lan hesitated.

"Well, blow me down! I forgot about the luggage." Uncle Bob ran his hand over his hair, thinning into a triangle over his forehead. "Lan, I'll need your strong right arm to help with it."

"Lan?" asked Aunt Jenny.

"Oh, I forgot to tell you," Uncle Bob twinkled. "When Lan was little he could say only the endings of words, so Alan became Lan."

While Uncle Bob and Lan waited for the luggage, Aunt Jenny sat in the old touring car. She had not long to wait.

"Here we are," said Uncle Bob cheerfully, dumping the luggage near the car, and then he and Lan stowed some of it carefully inside, and tied the rest on to a rack at the back. Lan stood staring at the "Old Bomb". He took out a pencil and a notebook and jotted down its number, 131313.

"It's very shiny and polished for an old car," he ventured at last.

"Hongi helped to polish it in your honour." His uncle cranked vigorously as he spoke.

"Hongi?"

"Yes, you'll like Hongi. He's a Maori boy of about fourteen, and he lives with his mother down the street from us. She's a widow, very kind, and anxious that Hongi should have a good education, and do well in life. He's a bright boy, that one, and should go far."

"Does he speak English?" Lan asked. "I can't speak anything else, except a bit of French."

"Too right. Better than we do, sometimes."

Lan climbed into the front seat beside his uncle, because his aunt, smiling broadly, was wedged in by luggage in the back.

"Hold on to your hats!" his uncle ordered.

The sun blazed down, the windscreen wipers rasped hoarsely but unnecessarily, an unseen cicada sang its metallic song, and with a lurch and a jerk they were off.

"I hereby name this car the Rolls-Noise." Lan's eyes twinkled at his uncle.

"Did you hear that, Jenny?" Uncle Bob shouted with laughter.

"It's most suitable," his wife called back, cheerfully.

"Why are the windscreen wipers going in all this sunshine?" Lan asked Uncle Bob.

"We-ell," his uncle drawled, "we had to get a warrant of fitness for her, and that insists that her windscreen wipers will function. Trouble is they won't stop, wet or fine, and when the engine is switched on, the windscreen wipers tick along, too."

"Your mother and father'll be leaving London to come here in about three months' time, won't they, Lan?"

Uncle Bob asked, keeping his eyes rigidly on the road.

"Yes, though Father's never sure of the exact time things will take when he has a top secret job. I didn't think I could persuade them to let me come out to New Zealand alone, but London was so bleak and cold. Suddenly the thought of the sun that we were missing—well, I guess it made them change their minds—" Lan broke off, and smiled happily.

A streamlined blue car streaked by.

Uncle Bob's eyes narrowed. "Now what is Bulke doing in that car?" he muttered to no one in particular.

Lan watched the disappearing car. "Do you know him?"

"Too right I know him. He's the purser on the *Golden Star*. I know the car, too, but it doesn't belong to him. I don't suppose he saw me, because he didn't bat an eyelid."

Lan said suddenly, "There's a lot of smuggling between England and the Continent—Dad used to talk about it. Is there any in New Zealand? I mean, if you're in the Customs you'd know about it, wouldn't you?"

His uncle was silent for a few minutes.

"There's smuggling, and I do know about it," he growled at length. "I suppose, as the son of a detective, you're interested in that sort of thing? You found some very good clues for your father, I remember he wrote to me. Well, if you can clear up this mystery you'll be a better man than your uncle." He drove in silence, chewing on his pipe.

"Napier is not one of the main ports, and I suppose they think they can smuggle diamonds in without anyone suspecting, when they put it across in a secondary port."

Uncle Bob's eyes narrowed as he watched the road. "Got to watch every little thing."

"You sound just like Dad. He spent most of his time trying to train me into keeping my eyes and ears open." Lan grinned, and stirring uneasily, he said, "I could do with a bath. Sitting still for days in an aeroplane sort of makes you want to be a horse and gallop about, as well as having a wash."

"How did your father work when he was starting on a new case? He became a detective after I came to New Zealand, so I didn't see him in action." Uncle Bob slowed down the car as he listened for Lan's reply.

"Well, he always said it was luck, but then he'd go to work and note down everything he could about the case. I remember he wrote pages once about the people of a village—to me it seemed mostly to be the ramblings of an old lady, who kept the village store. But Dad didn't find her long-winded."

"Did your mother complain about the time he spent enthralled with her conversation?" Aunt Jenny laughed.

"She certainly did! But she was smiling when she said it. She even spent some time matching cottons in that shop. Very strange, because she seldom had anything to do with sewing."

"I guess that's why he's such a successful detective," Uncle Bob growled. "He has a well-trained son to help him."

"Not to mention his wife," laughed Aunt Jenny. "Did he find what he wanted in that village?"

"Yes, it took days, and he didn't notice it until he was poring over his notes one night. Two people, one who had been in London, and one in the village—a man and a woman—looked quite different, but they had one characteristic in common. They both tapped the fingers of the right hand on the back of the left one when they were thinking."

"Well, what did that prove?" Aunt Jenny asked from the back seat.

"Nothing at all. Just that one man in London disappeared with some jewels, and could be traced towards that village, but he disappeared there, too. The only newcomer for years was a woman who had just arrived. She seemed to feel the cold and wore lots of woollens and scarves muffling her up. Said very little, and had a fairly deep voice. Just once or twice, when she was trying to think about the groceries, she tapped her right hand on the back of her left one. The shopkeeper noticed. It was no proof, but it was a clue."

"And a correct one?" Aunt Jenny held on to the back of the front seat, as the car jerked and spluttered.

"Oh, yes. Finally they caught the man disguised as a woman. So well disguised, that they'd never have guessed if he hadn't that give-away habit of tapping his right fingers on the back of his left hand."

"I'm full of suspicions about the diamond smuggling," Uncle Bob growled. "I don't know much about those people on the ships. I just suspect lots of them. It could be that I'm barking up the wrong tree. I can't get near enough to study every one I suspect."

Lan's eyes narrowed. His mind was leaping to meet the challenge of this new mystery. Sights and sounds and smells.

He remembered the case of a man who ate aniseed balls. Very few grown-ups eat them. Usually children. And the bank robbery, and the teller, who wasn't sure what the robber looked like, but later remembered a faint smell of aniseed when he smelled it again at the identification parade. By itself it proved nothing, but with other evidence it added up to a conviction for armed robbery.

"Yes," he said, half aloud, "I'll have to keep awake to all the sights and sounds and smells."

The fields were wide and yellowing in the sun. Lan stared at them as they rattled past.

"Admiring our farms?" Aunt Jenny asked. "Napier is very fertile. You'll like our fruit, Lan."

"Scrummy!" he said smiling briefly, and stifling a yawn of exhaustion. "The houses look strange, too. Spread out, with gardens. Colourful, aren't they? I like the red roofs, and the green ones, too. What are the roofs made of?"

"Corrugated iron, and coloured tiles mostly, but when we come to the more densely populated area of Napier you'll see the reinforced concrete, flat-roofed type. Lots of those since the terrible earthquake years ago, in 1931."

"I've heard about that," Lan said, sombrely. "New Zealand does go in for earthquakes, doesn't it?"

"They usually sound worse than they are," Aunt Jenny assured him.

"There are houses and playgrounds now on the parts that were pushed up out of the sea in 1931," Uncle Bob said.

"I must be alert," Lan thought, as he watched the houses and gardens. They seemed to be moving, as if on an assembly belt. "I must try to solve that mystery of the diamond smuggling. I must..." he said, as his sleepy thoughts came in little splashes. He forced his eyes open.

"Do many people know about the smuggling?" Lan asked.

"Not many. There have been rumours, of course, but they died down again. Trouble is that I'm too well known to investigate without being noticed. If you and Hongi could be on the lookout—mind you, no getting into trouble or into danger. Just tell me if you see or hear of anything interesting, and then leave the dirty work for grown men to handle."

Lan nodded. "Gosh, it's going to be wonderful in New Zealand. All this sun, and the wide, open fields—"

"Paddocks, they're called here," Aunt Jenny laughed.

Lan's eyes sparkled. "I've a lot to learn. We'll be right on the smuggling job, too. Just now I feel as if I could sleep for about a hundred years, but to-morrow—" For a moment he was almost wide awake. "That man in the blue car—the purser—"

His eyelids dropped, his brown head rested on the back of the seat, and Lan slept as the ancient car coughed its way home.

As he slept Lan muttered: "*Golden Star... Golden...*"

CHAPTER TWO

LAN AWOKE with the warmth of sunlight on his face. The birds were singing like an orchestra of tiny tin cans, and there was a smell of coffee mingled with toast. He could hear the sharp sound of a tap being turned on and off, and the gurgling of running water. It took him a few minutes to realise where he was, and he lay luxuriating in the glow of the sunlight on his face, the smooth softness of the sheets, and a feeling of excitement at the prospect of adventures to come.

He heard a scraping and a sliding of claws on the polished floor, and his eyelids flew open as if controlled by hidden springs.

"Here's Wuffit come to say good morning," his uncle, dressed in khaki shorts and an open-necked shirt, greeted him.

Lan looked down eagerly, and Wuffit, knowing what was expected of him, stood on his hind legs, and gravely proffered one paw. Lan shook the black paw, and studied the fawn and black, rough-haired, little mongrel.

"I can't decide what sort of dog he is," he said, at length.

"Part spaniel, part Alsatian, a dash of poodle, with a sprinkling of fox terrier," his uncle assured him gravely.

Lan shouted with laughter. "Not really?" he gasped.

"We-ell," drawled his uncle, "he might be anything. Really, he's just a plain, lovable dog."

19

The plain, lovable dog said, "Wuff!" once, sharply skidded across the room, and disappeared.

"He heard his bowl being put on the floor," Uncle Bob explained, with a smile.

"I could eat a horse myself." Lan sprang out of bed. "Be ready in no time!"

After breakfast Lan helped to clear the table and dried the dishes.

"Thank you, Lan." Aunt Jenny wiped down the bench. "Uncle Bob doesn't go to work to-day, as he has holidays. He's going to weed the garden and fix bits of the Rolls-Noise. You may play now, if you like. We'll take you to the Mardi Gras later. There's always a Mardi Gras in Napier at Christmas and New Year."

A sudden knock on the back door interrupted her.

"Ah, that'll be Hongi." She opened the door. "Come and meet Lan." A tall Maori boy followed her into the kitchen.

Grey eyes met dark brown eyes with quick awareness. Lan stared curiously at Hongi, and Hongi, with equal interest, stared back. Lan saw a boy, taller than him-self, bronze-brown, with gleaming teeth, and a wide, friendly smile. He saw a faded shirt, patterned with sailing ships, and too-short shorts. He noted the lithe, athletic strength before him and secretly envied the mixture of outdoorlife, sun and freedom that had built Hongi.

Hongi, in turn, saw the tall, thin, rather bony boy, with paleness from an indoor life, and the easy confidence that comes from a careful home and school training. He envied the polish of such an upbringing, but would not have changed with it.

"What does your name mean, Hongi?" Lan said in his clipped, English voice, as he smiled a greeting.

A wide grin spread over Hongi's face, lighted up his eyes, and ended in a burst of sudden laughter. Before Lan realised what was happening, Hongi ran to him, and pressed his nose against Lan's.

"That's what Hongi means," he said, grinning at Lan's astonishment. "It's a nose-pressing—a Maori greeting."

Lan laughed back. "Well, I asked for it, but I've never seen—or felt—anything like that before."

"Lan seems a strange name to me," Hongi said.

"Well, it's just short for Alan."

Lan and Hongi smiled with the suppressed excitement of those who will enjoy adventures together.

"By the way, the shed is a playhouse for both of you, when you want to have secret meetings," Uncle Bob laughed. "You could use the bench as a work bench, or as a desk when you're writing up important statements."

"Let's have a secret society!" Hongi's eyes gleamed.

Lan took a quick step forward. "Smugglers! We'll start a junior branch of the C.I.D."

"In New Zealand it's the C.I.B.—Criminal Investigation Branch—and I'm sure they'll be delighted when they hear of their junior branch," Uncle Bob laughed.

"Now, don't tease them, Bob," said Aunt Jenny moving towards the door.

"We'll keep our junior C.I.B. a secret," Lan grinned. "The grown-up C.I.B. will be the last to know."

"I have an urgent appointment with an apple pie," said Aunt Jenny and she hurried towards the kitchen.

"It's more serious than it looks, boys." Uncle Bob shut the door carefully, and sat down on an up-ended apple case.

"Smugglers?" Lan's eyes narrowed.

"It's not general knowledge, and the less that leaks out the better..."

"We won't say a word," Lan and Hongi assured him together.

Uncle Bob carefully filled his pipe.

"We suspect they're using Napier to smuggle in diamonds, but we don't know for sure. As customs men we've checked everything as carefully as we can, but short of ripping everything to bits, and that's not possible unless we get a lead on what to rip, we-ell—" He ran his hand over his hair, smoothing it as he spoke, and then rumpling it wildly as he came to no conclusion.

"Does it happen more often at any particular time?" Lan asked, with poised pencil.

"Yes, usually at Christmas and at New Year." His uncle started doodling on a piece of wood with one of the pencils.

Lan stiffened like a hunting dog tensed for action. Somewhere he remembered something—something that eluded him now.

Hongi took up a notebook and a pencil, and jotted notes on the facts as they knew them. He was suddenly quiet and alert.

Uncle Bob stood up. "You may be able to help, boys. Somewhere you might be able to pick up a clue that we haven't noticed. But no running into danger, mind. You're both too valuable to risk in any way. And don't you forget it!"

When Uncle Bob had left them Hongi and Lan looked thoughtfully at each other.

"Senior Detective Hongi, you be in charge." Lan ran his fingers through his dark hair.

"We'll both be in charge, Senior Detective Lan."

"Aided and abetted by Flying Officer Wuffit," Lan interrupted, with a grin. "I don't think there are flying officers in the C.I.B., but a dashing dog like Wuffit would just have to be a flying officer! We'll look for clues, and keep our eyes open. Father often told me how—he's a detective. You try to notice everything—sounds, smells, the feeling of things, mannerisms, tones of voice and so on. Most of them, by themselves, aren't important, but added up we might get something."

Thoughtfully they went into the garden.

"I wonder what the other children are doing now?" came a high, complaining and penetrating whisper from the other side of the fence.

"No one ever asks us to play. Wow! She kicked me first! Take that! And that!" a boy's voice shouted, angrily. There was a loud howl of anguish.

"Children! Children!" a woman's voice called. "Stop quarrelling. Try to enjoy your holiday."

"We are enjoying our holiday! You little—! I'll teach you to throw your bucket at me!"

Lan's eyebrows went up in an unspoken question.

Hongi's lips formed the words, as he whispered almost soundlessly: "They're Sis and Bruffie, the terrible twins. They visit their aunt once a year. I think it takes her the rest of the year to recover."

"That's a lie!" came floating over the fence. "She got a far bigger piece of apple than I did. It's not fair. No one ever gives us fair shares. Eow! Eow! She's bitten me!"

"Aw, let's forget them," Hongi shrugged with disgust. "They never enjoy anything, unless they're hurting someone." He picked up a stick and threw it for Wuffit to fetch. The furry Wuffit raced after it, retrieved it carefully, dropped it at Hongi's feet, and stood back with eager panting and hanging tongue, waiting for it to be thrown again.

As Hongi threw the stick over and over again, Lan wandered off, watching and thinking. He saw sweet-peas, dahlias, roses and sweet williams, that he knew in England, and studied the other flowers, purple, magenta and scarlet, that were new to him. The warm scents of the garden lay on the silent air, and in the insect world the beetles, the ants and the butterflies were busy under the cloudless sky of the Napier morning.

And somewhere at the back of his mind the clue eluded him.

Suddenly he gave a wild shout. "I've got it, Hongi!" He raced back to Hongi, now lying under the walnut tree. "I've got it!"

Hongi opened one eye, and shut it again.

"Aunt Jenny told us that there's a Mardi Gras in Napier every year at Christmas and New Year."

"So what?" Hongi settled his dark, curly head more comfortably on his arm.

"Don't you see? The smuggling goes on then—at Christmas and New Year. Perhaps it's a clue!"

Hongi sat up with a jerk. "Well, jumping cricket bats! You might have something there."

CHAPTER THREE

CLUES

UNCLE BOB turned off the garden tap, and coiled the hose under it.

"There! The car's clean enough now. We have a spring under that tap, boys," he said to Lan and Hongi. He lifted the bonnet of the Rolls-Noise, and peered inside.

"Uncle Bob?"

"Uh?" he asked, after a time, as if he had just heard Lan's voice.

"I only wanted to know if Hongi and I could go to the Mardi Gras this afternoon? That is, if it's all right with you and Aunt Jenny." Lan gazed with interest at the car engine.

His uncle started to rub his hand through his hair, as he usually did when thinking.

"Ugh! I forgot my hands were greasy," he smiled ruefully, and wiped them instead on some cotton waste.

Lan waited, comparing his uncle's old khaki shorts and holiday-faded sports shirt with the bowler-hatted, rolled-umbrella men, who hurried past their house in London every morning and evening.

"I was wondering," Uncle Bob said slowly, "if you'd do a job for me this afternoon. We could go to the Mardi Gras to-night. It's lasting a few weeks longer than usual this year, too. But later this afternoon, when it's cooler, it might be useful if you went fishing from the wharves."

Lan and Hongi opened their eyes wide with surprise. Lan turned his head slightly to one side, watching.

"Oh, I don't think you'd catch much fish. I don't mean useful in that way." Uncle Bob looked round before he spoke again, and lowered his voice into a deep, bass rumble. "The *Golden Star* is there now. You could go fishing from one of the wharves—lots of boys do that— and keep an eye open, without saying anything about your real business there. If I take a stroll along the wharf you don't know me, and I don't know you. Understand?"

"Sure thing," Hongi grinned.

"I, myself, have to read a book called *Detection and Crime*. Very useful, too," Uncle Bob twinkled.

"Well," Lan said, "that leaves Flying Officer Wuffit."

"Flying Officer Wuffit believes in a siesta in the hotter parts of the day," Uncle Bob assured them.

"Good. That allows us to work together in greater secrecy and peace," Lan grinned, wriggling his bare toes in his sandals.

"Ask your mother if you may go, Hongi, and if she says yes, join Lan here after lunch, about two o'clock. She might allow you to walk up Bluff Hill, if you have time."

"Thank you, Mr. Sherwood. I'll ask her." Hongi rubbed his right big toe on his left ankle in pleased antici- pation. "But I'm sure she'll say it's all right." His teeth gleamed with delight.

When Hongi left, running quietly with a little skip at every sixth step, Lan spent half an hour before lunch learning about the engine in the Rolls-Noise.

"Can you stop a car being stolen, Uncle Bob?"

"They usually call it converting a car—though why one thing can be stolen and another converted beats me.

You want to know what to do if someone tries to take the Rolls-Noise?"

"Yes," Lan agreed.

His uncle laughed. "Well, first of all, think of the noise! I doubt if anyone would want to take a car that coughs and groans so loudly. Might as well shout 'I'm a stolen car' and have done with it."

Lan laughed, too. "But how do you stop them?" he persisted.

"Well, this part I've opened up here is the distributor, and this little fellow in the middle is the rotor. No one could take the car if you removed the rotor. Not unless they carry spare rotors to fit, that is, and that's not likely."

"Bob! Lan! Lunch is ready!" Aunt Jenny stood in the doorway, smiling a warm, comfortable smile, as if she had everything in the whole world to please her.

Together Uncle Bob and Lan crossed to the house, where the sharp scent of baking apples mingled with the buttery smell of pastry, and hot, spicy cloves.

The sudden spurt of water from the tap, and the splashing into the basin as Lan washed his hands, broke the breathing silence of the deep, midday heat.

After lunch Lan sat down on the porch in the shade, and slowly and deliberately thought of this new country so far away from London. The crackle of dry paper, the stiff, dry clothes on the clothes-lines, the withering lawn, all showed the dehydrating process that seemed part of this summer heat. He looked at all the fruit trees in the garden—lemons, walnuts, apples, grapes, peaches, nectarines, apricots, and the still-green passion-fruit, climbing over the garage.

Mum and Dad would like it a lot, he thought. "You know," he told Aunt Jenny, "I've never lived in a place where the fruit grew like this before. Until I asked I didn't even know the names of most of the trees. After living in London it's wonderful to have your own fruit in your own garden, Aunt Jenny. Just smashing."

Aunt Jenny's eyes crinkled, and she laughed. "I remember when we first came to live here I found it very hot, but what amazed me most of all were the dishes. They were always warm in the cupboard, as if they had been washed in hot water and newly dried."

"I suppose everyone sees the same things differently. What did Uncle Bob notice?"

"We-ell," Uncle Bob came through the screen door in time to hear Lan's words, "I guess I noticed the modern cars, most of all. Hawkes Bay is a rich farming district— hence the cars, I suppose."

"Hongi sees things differently again," Aunt Jenny leaned forward to watch a huge, orange Monarch butter-fly dip and soar and glide. "Hongi used to make my hair stand on end with his insect collection. He says Napier is wonderful for watching insects. He's very kind about the insects, too. Waits till they die, before he collects them. Doesn't like to kill them. He seems fond of them, like we feel about Wuffit. People have sent him insects from all over the place."

"I like his giraffe beetle, a weevil, best of them all. It's six and a half inches long, Lan, and has a long snout for boring holes in dead trees."

"Yes," said Aunt Jenny settling back into the creaking cane chair, now that the butterfly was out of sight. "But the oddest of them is the stick insect. Just you wait till you see a dry looking old twig moving slowly like a robot, Lan. That'll make you sit up!"

"It certainly will," Lan agreed. "I've a lot to learn. I don't know a thing about insects."

"Here's Hongi, now," Uncle Bob pulled out his pipe. "Judging by his delighted expression and the fishing rod—I'll have to get you one, when the shops open—he's allowed to go."

Uncle Bob took a long draw on his pipe. Hongi sat down and stuck out his feet.

"I'm wearing my sandals this afternoon. Did you know that it's ninety degrees to-day, Mr. Sherwood? The bitumen on the road's melting. Too hot to walk on in bare feet, anyway."

Uncle Bob nodded slowly. "Too right," he said. "Now, about the fishing on the wharves—just act as naturally as you can, and keep your ears and eyes open. You mightn't find out a thing, but I'm suspicious of some of the crew on those ships."

"Why the crew? Why not the passengers?" Lan asked, intense with concentration.

"We-ell, it could be passengers, I suppose, but it's happened fairly regularly when certain ships are in port, and the *Golden Star* is one of them. I've had a good look at passenger lists, and I may have slipped up somewhere, but I can't get a line on them anywhere." He puffed at his pipe for a few moments before he spoke again.

"While you're on the wharves take a look at Bluff Hill. It might be quite important. It looks over the wharves. It's steep and cut off sheer at the edge of the cliff. There's an enormous cactus growing just below the hill top, and the concrete lookout is above and to the left of it. But don't get into danger. If you go up Bluff Hill, you'll know not to climb the fence at the edge. You'd be goners if you fell down that cliff."

"We'll be careful—" Hongi began.

He was interrupted by a scream that grew louder and louder. Over the fence came Sis's voice, shrill with indignation.

"I did not! He kicked me first!"

"Your peach is bigger than mine. Take that!" came Bruffie's snarl of rage.

A metal catch grated as a window was pushed open.

"Come inside!"

"Won't, you old meanie. You never let us do anything!"

Uncle Bob rose abruptly. His fingers drummed on the back of his chair.

"If it's the last thing I do," he muttered, "I'll fix those twins. They haven't a grateful bone in their bodies." He knocked his pipe out with savage, staccato taps. He turned to Lan and Hongi. "Now, if you see me this afternoon on the wharf or anywhere, you don't know me, and I don't know you. And if you should see a tape recorder in the garden, well, you just didn't see it at all. None as blind as those who don't want to see."

"Aye, aye, sir." Hongi clicked his sandals together sharply, and saluted with military precision. His teeth, surrounded by an expanse of pink gums, showed in a widening grin.

Senior Detectives Hongi and Lan strolled over the lawn to the Junior Criminal Investigation Branch Head-quarters. Flying Officer Wuffit hurled himself in joyous frenzy between their legs.

"No, Wuffit, we're going to work. Play later." Lan patted Wuffit's tousled head, and was rewarded by a loud breathing of panting devotion.

The headquarters shed was cool, although a shaft of hot sunlight arrowed through its spiderweb-festooned windows. Lan drew up an apple box to the bench, and tapped a notebook with his ball-point pen.

"Shouldn't we write in invisible ink?" asked Hongi settling beside him on another apple box.

"If we do, we won't be able to re-read it, or study it without making it visible first," Lan said slowly.

"Well, what about noting down all relevant material— doesn't that sound well? I got it out of a book on detection—and re-write the main points in invisible ink later?"

"Good idea." Lan chewed his pen, thoughtfully. "What do we know?"

"We know nothing," Hongi assured him gloomily.

"We suspect that something happens at the time of the Mardi Gras."

"Too right. And some ship has something to do with it. Perhaps the *Golden Star.* Perhaps all sorts of red herrings to cover up the smuggling."

Lan stood up, and in the manner of a dog padding in circles before he lies down on grass, he stalked round and round, thinking before he sat down again.

"Hm!" Hongi watched him, grinning.

"I do the oddest things when I'm thinking," Lan confessed, sheepishly. "Don't realise I'm doing them, half the time. I'll try to reform." He wandered on to the lawn.

Hongi paced the short length of the shed. "Let's get off and see what we can find out at the wharves. We can always write this up later. Oh, I forgot—" he moved to the lawn, and paused.

"What's the matter, Hongi?" Lan looked up as Hongi's shadow halted beside him. "You look as cheerful as a camel that's going to be taken for a ride in a bus."

"Cheerful?" growled Hongi. "Why should I be cheerful? Of all the things to blight a holiday?" Words failed him.

"You haven't told me yet what's biting you," said Lan, drawing down the corners of his mouth in an imitation of Hongi's.

"My cousin, Thomasina, arrived for a holiday in Napier last night. I saw her at lunch time." Hongi gave an angry kick to the grass.

"Is that all?" Lan laughed.

"All?" Hongi groaned hollowly. "My red-headed cousin Thomasina—not my first cousin, but my sixth-cousin twice-removed, or something like that—is more trouble than twenty monkeys escaped from the zoo. She just can't do anything right. At least, I don't think so. And what's worse, she follows me round, sort of prowling."

"And you don't like that?"

"That's putting it mildly." Hongi succeeded in kicking a clump of grass several feet.

"Perhaps we can avoid her," said Lan as he aimed a peach stone at the shed.

"Perhaps we can't." Hongi refused all comfort. "She's not staying with us, but she's staying with her fashionable aunt. No relation of mine. And that means that Thomasina is more or less on the loose while the aunt gives advice in her beauty salon on how to brighten up your appearance by wearing pink wigs and purple lip-stick. You know the sort of thing? Makes me sick," Hongi growled. "And people pay for it!"

"Perhaps she won't find you here."

"She'll ferret me out. She won't have anything else to do. She always finds me because she thinks I might be in the middle of an adventure." Suddenly he laughed. "Last year Thomasina went to a finishing school."

"Is she old enough for that? I didn't know they had finishing schools in New Zealand."

"She's thirteen. But I didn't mean the school finished Thomasina. I meant she finished the school. They had a hobbies course, or a pets' session, if you wanted to do that instead. The chairman of the school committee offered a prize for the best one—the one who had done the most work, and had shown originality, and had added generally to the tone and culture of the school. They had to write an account of what they had done." Hongi gave a sudden guffaw of laughter.

They wandered over to the shed. "Thomasina's essay was outstanding. I read it myself." They closed the shed door, and sat down on up-ended apple boxes.

"Did she get the prize?"

"Not exactly, but when they heard about the difficulty she had in collecting her pets, how she was going to make them love her, and train them, well, they decided to give her a prize for diligence."

There was a bloodcurdling shriek and a sudden thump, as of a heavy object falling on piled up fruit boxes and rubbish tins. Hongi and Lan together catapulted from the shed.

"My bicycle!" howled Hongi, in anger.

"You must be Thomasina!" Lan lifted the bicycle from the redheaded girl entangled between the crossbar and the wheels.

Slowly she rose, slowly she shook her flaming red hair out of her eyes, and slowly she smiled. "So there you are, Hongi," she said, sweetly. "I knew I'd find you. I always do."

"And why," demanded Hongi, "didn't you tell Mom that you couldn't ride a bike before she lent you mine?"

"Because," Thomasina smiled with the tolerance of one explaining to the very young, "she wouldn't have lent it if she had known that."

In complete silence Hongi kicked a clump of grass until it broke into twenty pieces against the side of the shed.

"Girls!" Hongi growled. "Not that I have anything against other girls, only against Thomasina."

"Our ancestor, Thomas Moriarty, was a whaler," Thomasina explained suddenly to Lan, in the well-bred tones of one who has benefitted from speech lessons. "He married a Maori princess first of all, and when she died he married a Scottish girl, daughter of a miner. Hongi was descended from the Maori princess, and I from the miner's daughter."

"Hongi was telling me about the prize you got for diligence with your pets."

"Oh," said Thomasina, deflated. "I was going to make them love me—"

"They'd love you at every bite," Hongi assured her.

"And at the prize-giving it seemed such a shame to have them all shut up—"

"So she let them out on the platform. I'll never forget it," Hongi chuckled. "The headmistress looked sort of stricken, as if she couldn't bear to move. Then she gave a sudden twist and scratched vigorously. A bishop was seated with his hands folded across his stomach, intent on the uplifting speeches. Uplifting! I'll say they were! Some of the important people on that platform even bounced!"

Thomasina chortled, and she and Hongi rolled on the lawn with roars of laughter.

"I had to apologise to them all, separately, afterwards," Thomasina confessed ruefully. "But the bishop was a pet. He's a dear old man, awf'lly old, actually, bald, and with a face like a withered, rosy apple. 'My dear child,' he said, so no one could hear, 'in my long life I've been to many, many prize-givings. But none like this, I assure you.' I'm sure there was a twinkle in his eye. 'And strangely, my gaiters seem to have saved me from the onslaught.'"

"Surely they could have caught your pets, and put them outside," Lan suggested.

"Caught them?" Hongi sat up for a moment. "Caught them? That would have been better still! But I don't think even the bishop himself would be much good at catching performing fleas!"

CHAPTER FOUR

"I SUPPOSE," Hongi said, as they set out, with fishing rod and bait, after Thomasina had gone home, "that we should find something to use for invisible ink."

"We've a lemon tree in the garden, so it should be easy." Lan swung the tin of bait as he walked. "Golly, this is a scorcher of a day, isn't it?"

They walked in step, rhythmically, and sang snatches of sea chanties as they strode along. Hongi pushed his battered straw sunhat back on his head and wiped his forehead.

"Vauxhall." Hongi gazed ahead. A Vauxhall car shot past.

"Chev." Hongi gave his attention to the footpath.

"Gosh!" Lan gasped. "How can you tell? You didn't even look at them."

"I know the sound of the engines. They all have a different sort of voice."

"Golly!" Lan listened carefully. "What's coming now?"

"Bentely, I think."

"Caught you out. It's a vintage car. Certainly not a Bentley, though I didn't get a good look at the bonnet."

"Hm-m!" Hongi looked completely unconcerned, even not interested. "I've never yet made a mistake about a car engine," he said, quietly.

36

Lan laughed, sceptically, as he turned and noted the luxuriant growth in the gardens, which were not yet dried up in spite of the heat. The soil was gritty and sandy and finely textured. He stopped to look at it more closely.

Hongi paused, too. "This part of Napier was pushed up out of the sea in the earthquake of 1931. Plants grow well here."

He pointed out the lines of enormous Phoenix palms, symbols of the new Napier rising from the ashes of the old.

"The palms give a tropical appearance to the street," Lan said, "and they look a bit odd growing side by side with English trees."

"Can't say I've noticed it before. Just took them for granted," said Hongi staring at the trees.

When they reached the wharves, where a number of children were fishing, they wandered silently in what seemed to be an aimless fashion. They paused where the *Golden Star* was berthed.

"Good place for fishing," Hongi said, loudly. Without moving his lips he added, "Just here, Lan, and we can keep an eye on anyone coming from that ship."

"Jolly good fishing here," Lan agreed loudly, as if he knew something about it. "Do you know anything about the history of Napier?" he asked with ringing clarity.

"I know an awful lot," Hongi grinned modestly. "We had to do a social survey on it at school last year, and believe me we left out nothing. Thought old Fiddlesticks, that's our teacher, would have nightmares about it by the time he'd listened to forty separate accounts of the place, and marked forty social studies."

"Conscientious type?" Lan laughed. "I can just see him. Tall and thin—"

"Not on your life! Short and fat, and plays the violin surprisingly well. Hence Fiddlesticks." He lowered his voice, "Keep your eyes open."

"I don't know a thing about Napier," Lan said loudly in his clipped English voice.

"Well, I'll tell you, and I'll try not to frighten the fish."

"What fish?" Lan asked, with dancing eyes.

Hongi ignored him, and announced: "In 1769 it was sighted by Captain Cook."

"Oh," Lan bent and fiddled with the fishing line.

"A chap named Rhodes started a trading station about sixty years later, but the Maori soon put a stop to that by burning it down. Four or five years later—that'd be in about the eighteen forties—the first white settler, William Colenso, came."

With unmoving lips Lan said, "Someone's coming off the ship now."

They concentrated on their task of baiting the line, and Lan bent still lower as a tall, gaunt man in captain's uniform stepped on to the wharf. He looked about, and took off his cap to fan his face. Lan, glancing up, stood for a second as if transfixed. Not a single hair adorned the smooth dome of the captain's head. Not an eyebrow nor an eyelash ruffled the surface of his parchment-like face.

Lan remembered the bait, and hastily turned away. A thin man, sharp nosed, with a long, stringy-looking neck adorned with a fluttering orange tie, and wearing a grey sports coat and grey flannel trousers, joined the captain. Together they came towards the two boys.

"Might as well look in at the Mardi Gras," the captain said to his companion.

"Might be something worth our while there," said the other giving a high squeak of laughter.

As if a rat were laughing, Lan thought, turning away. He saw the railway tracks on the wharf, the concrete building at the far end, the huge searchlights. Turning, his eyes travelled up the steep cliff beyond the road, saw the giant cactus, and peered to see the lookout above it.

"Is that Bluff Hill?" he asked Hongi, softly.

"Yes." Hongi suddenly seemed engrossed in studying the water. He squatted, silent and tense, his brown eyes fixed on the rise and fall of the sea, and Lan, not daring to look up again, kneeled, busying himself with the bait.

"It goes like this," a harsh voice above him hummed a few bars. Another, a light tenor, tried to catch the tune, and failed. He attempted it once more, and this time he was successful. The captain and the man in grey passed without a glance towards the boys, so industriously fishing nearby.

As the men walked they hummed softly, in unison, and as he listened, Lan remembered the tune. He had often heard it in London. Its catchy rhythm seemed to belong with the ebb of the waves, and before he realised what he was doing, Lan whistled a few bars. The bald-headed man wheeled, as if shot, and stared suspiciously at the boys fishing, but shrugged as he saw their preoccupation with their rod and bait.

"Must be hearing things," he growled. "I could have sworn—" He and his companion left the wharf without another backward glance.

Hongi looked up, and as quickly looked down again.

As if unintentionally he moved closer to Lan. "By crikey, you nearly put your foot in it that time, Lan," he muttered with quiet lips. "What's the tune?"

Lan's face was like a mask, expressionless, disinterested. "'The Roundabout'. There's a merry-go-round at the Mardi Gras, isn't there?" Aloud, he said, "Fishing's not too good this afternoon. You'd think the fish would come near a ship to get scraps of food. You haven't told me all about Napier. Why was it called that, and—"

"After Sir Charles Napier. He was famous in the Battle of Meeanee in the Indian Province of Scinde. At one time Napier was on an island, Scinde Island, and two shingle spits ran out from it. They reclaimed a lot of land, and then the big earthquake of 1931 pushed up more land. Eight feet in some places."

"It's got quite a history," Lan commented.

"Too right. There was a terrific fire after the earthquake, and it burnt down all the shops and that part of the town, so that it looks pretty new now, because so much had to be rebuilt."

"I want to learn all I can about the places I see. Dad also believes in knowing what happened in the past, so that we can link it up with the present, and be that much more interested in places."

"Of course all this is new to you, but I hadn't much idea of things until we had to do that social survey at school. Old Fiddlesticks is barmy about social studies. Joins digging parties when they're looking for moa bones and things."

"Moa bones?"

"Yes. Moas were those huge birds, with long necks, and no wings. They had died out before the white men came

to New Zealand. Well, old Fiddlesticks has a couple of
crossed moa bones—huge things bigger than the leg
bones of a cow—hung over the mantelpiece in his lounge
at home."

"We had a master like that at school, but he went in
for Roman remains, and followed in the footsteps of the
Vikings when he wasn't yelling at us," Lan grinned.
"Shocking temper had old Fossilwit."

"Still pretty hot, isn't it?" Hongi gazed into the cool
depths of the sea. "Could do with a swim, but we'd better
sort of linger about for a while, and see if we can get any
information for your uncle."

"I'd give a bit to know what they use that 'Roundabout'
tune for." Absent-mindedly Lan hummed a few bars as
he moved his arms in time to the rhythm.

"There you go again," Hongi laughed.

"What was I doing? I was only thinking."

"Yes, but you do all sorts of odd things when you're
thinking. Remember?"

"What was I doing this time?"

"It could have been a shadow dance, or conducting an
invisible orchestra, or—"

"Oh, stow it, Hongi. I must have looked an utter fool!"

"You did!"

He ducked carefully as Lan aimed, and threw a piece of
bait at him.

"What say we go for a tramp, instead?"

Hongi nodded, briefly, and they packed up their gear,
strolled down to the end of the wharf, and casually wandered back again.

"Any luck, Hongi?" a boy in khaki shorts and a gaily
coloured shirt called.

"No. We're going for a bit of a hike now," Hongi paused, and Lan strolled ahead.

"You'll find it a swelter. Tell you what, though. I'll drop your gear in at your place on the way past. My old man is going to pick me up at about four."

"Why, thanks, Jimmy, that'd help a lot," Hongi said handing the fishing line to him. "You can have the bait if you can use it."

"I don't expect those crazy fish to be biting a lot," Jimmy laughed. "But thanks all the same."

Hongi caught up with Lan, and they sauntered along the wharf. Then Hongi looked back, and his eyes swept along past the people fishing, and beyond them to the still, deep water. He looked towards the *Golden Star*, lying idle, as if painted, on that rippled sea.

Suddenly Hongi was running towards the end of the wharf, tearing off his shirt as he ran.

Lan sprang after him, tense and questioning. His breath came in little gulping gasps from a listening, bottled-up excitement. Then he saw why Hongi was running—running as if his life depended on it.

In the sea, astern of the *Golden Star*, a head was bobbing, and one uplifted arm was waving frantically.

As he watched, Lan saw the head and the arm disappear under the engulfing water, and at the same moment Hongi dived, slid through the water like a brown spear, and struck out towards the place where the head had disappeared.

"Help! Man overboard!" Lan shouted at the top of his voice. He felt a hot, angry, rising frustration. If only he could swim like Hongi he'd be of some use. Later he'd definitely get Hongi to teach him. As it was, he could swim a few yards in shallow water, but would be useless in an emergency of this sort. He ran to the steps at the end of the wharf.

Hongi was nearing the place where the man had disappeared, but there was now no sign of the head and the waving arm in the water. A group of children joined Lan, and watched silently and helplessly. There seemed to be no grown-ups to help, no little boats within sight, only a group of frightened children.

As Hongi dived to search, the children suddenly came to life, as if freed from some witch's spell of silence. With one voice they shouted, "Help! Help! HELP!"

There were feet hurrying now. Heavy, dull footsteps of men running along the wharf.

Lan watched, holding his breath as Hongi dived again. Somewhere a motor-boat started up. The thud of its engine kept time with Lan's thumping heart and gasping breath.

"He's got him!" a child screamed, and they all took up the shout, "He's got him!" as Hongi turned on to his back, and began to tow an inert form. The seconds lengthened into minutes, and the minutes of waiting seemed like hours. A piece of cloth tore away in Lan's hands, and he looked down in surprise to see his handkerchief, shredded and useless, clutched tightly in his fingers.

"I didn't even know I was ripping it," he muttered, as he gazed out to sea again.

Hongi paused, and a sigh went up from the children, "He's getting tired. He won't make it—yes, he will—he's starting again—"

The motor-boat drew closer, and the throb of the engine stopped suddenly.

"Gosh! His engine's conked out!" a child gasped.

Hongi paused again to rest, and the children shouted, "You're nearly there! You're nearly there! Come on! COME ON!"

The phut! phut! of the motor-boat came again on the hot air, and as the children on the wharf steps put down eager hands to help Hongi and to relieve him of his burden, the motor-boat throbbed back to the wharf.

Lan never could have told afterwards how they dragged Hongi and his unconscious burden out of the water, and up the steps, but suddenly he knew he was moving the seaman on to his back, with his head turned to the side.

"Clear foreign matter," Lan muttered to himself. "Head backwards, chin forward. Close his mouth." He placed his own widely-opened mouth over the seaman's nostrils and blew deeply and regularly.

Hongi, exhausted, panted with weary gasps as he lay on the wharf. The water, dripping off his clothes, soon dried in the hot sun.

The seaman stirred, but Lan went on blowing deeply and regularly.

A voice said, "He's all right now, sonny. He'll be fine now. We'll get him on board, and he'll be as right as rain."

Lan smiled, and was given the ghost of an answering smile by the seaman, who seemed too dazed to speak.

"Hongi saved you, really," he said, and Hongi, hearing his name, opened his eyes and grinned as the seaman was borne off by the men, who had been in the motor-boat, and by another stranger, who had suddenly appeared.

"That's the doctor," a child near Lan explained.

Hongi roasted one side in the hot sun, then turned over to his other side. His clothes steamed gently.

"What'll we do now?" he asked, stirring at last.

"Well, gosh, haven't you done enough?" Lan asked in amazement.

"I don't want to go home so early in the day," Hongi explained. "If Mum heard what had happened she'd think I ought to go straight to bed to have a rest." He snorted in derision. "Bed! On a day like this!"

Lan laughed softly. They stood up, and strolled along the wharf.

"Perhaps we should wait here a bit longer," Hongi said softly as they reached the *Golden Star*. "After all, I can gently steam dry in the sun, and you can think, in your queer way, of this and that."

"Hm!" Lan growled, glowering.

"We might get some clues, eh?" Hongi squatted down, and then lay full length on the wharf. Lan crouched beside him, tracing circles with his fingers on the rubber fenders at the edge.

"About that car," Hongi turned lazily, "the one you laughed about. The vintage one."

"What about it?"

"It was a Bentley." Hongi turned on his side, and pretended to sleep. He ignored Lan's hoot of disbelief.

The minutes passed in the semi-maze of a summer's day. The *Golden Star* seemed embedded in the glassy sea.

"I feel half asleep," Hongi muttered. "Wake me up if I begin to snore, Lan."

"Here's something that'll wake you up. Don't look up, but Thomasina and Uncle Bob are coming. She's dancing up and down beside him, showing how bright and gay a girl can be when she wants to impress everyone with the time she's having."

"Drat Thomasina," Hongi said kindly.

"Uncle Bob's striding along in his old shorts, as if he were on a tramping tour."

"Hm-m!" Hongi settled more comfortably, and warmed the other side of his damp T-shirt.

Uncle Bob did not glance in their direction. He was busy pointing out the different ships to the girl skipping at his side.

"We'll wait until they're out of the way, and then let's go for our interrupted hike," Lan said softly, gazing into the sea, so gently lapping the sides of the *Golden Star.*

"Good-o," Hongi agreed.

"They're stopping near the end of the wharf," said Lan, turning slightly. He watched his uncle with eyes narrowed against the light. "Oh, bother those boys near the steps. They're pointing us out, and obviously telling Uncle all about that seaman."

"Seems we can't keep anything to ourselves," Hongi sat up. "I'd better look alive and kicking, or Thomasina will think I need the gentle ministrations of a snooping sixth cousin."

"They couldn't appear less interested," Lan assured him. Then softly, "They're passing us on their way back, now. We'll let them get away, and then, if there's nothing doing here, off we go."

They stood up, and turned towards the road.

"Hallo. Hallo-o, there! You boys!" A voice hailed them across the water.

They looked about them, startled. Then an arm, waving from the *Golden Star* attracted their attention.

"It's the bloke who fell into the water," Hongi muttered.

"Come and see over the *Golden Star* next time you're down on the wharf!" the seaman shouted, in a rather tired voice.

Two other seamen joined him, and hurried him away.

"Guess they're hustling him back to bed," Hongi's teeth showed in a widening grin.

"He wants to show us over the *Golden Star*," Lan muttered, half to himself. "The *Golden Star*! I wonder if it's safe to go on board."

CHAPTER FIVE

BLUFF HILL

SLOWLY THEY returned along Breakwater Road to Coote Road, and set off for Bluff Hill. The smell of the sea was still sharp in the air as they paused to look at an ancient cannon outside an army office.

"Is the hill very steep?" Lan asked, after a few minutes.

"No, it's not, but we'll have to walk on the right side of the road when there's no footpath." Hongi looked carefully both ways. "My traffic warden training," he explained, with a broad grin. "They're keen on it at school. There's a Chev. coming."

Lan checked with a quick glance as a car passed. It was a Chevrolet.

The sun shone down hotly, giving a golden freshness to the leaves. The road began to mount more steeply, and from the lush growth in the gardens came the smell of flowers. They had turned from Coote Road, and were now stepping over the joins in a paving-block path.

When they reached Lighthouse Road, Lan and Hongi walked slowly, not talking. Lan felt strange in this Christmas weather of glaring sun, and thought of the snow on London streets. With an effort he jerked his thoughts back to the present, and became aware of dark haired Hongi trudging beside him; and then of the grape-fruit ripening in the gardens; and poppies and roses; and unknown purple and pink-orange flowers, highlighted with the clean, uncluttered beauty of the creeping blue convolvulus.

"I think," Hongi paused and listened, "that I heard a tui. Its note is rather like a bell." They listened, but the song was not repeated. "There's a Humber coming up the hill," Hongi remarked as he padded on silently. "It's stopped now."

The road narrowed, and grew cooler under the branches of overhanging trees.

"We're nearly there." Hongi took off his sunhat, and fanned his brown face. "It's only about a mile, or a mile and a half, from the wharves. Of course, on a hot day, it seems much farther. This detective business takes a bit of doing, doesn't it?"

They crossed over a grassy reserve to the lookout, as he spoke.

"It certainly—" Lan stopped suddenly, and started, his eyes hardening as a blue car swept past. Then, with his face like a mask, he crossed over to the fence, and gazed nonchalantly at the wharves far below. Hongi, taking his cue from Lan, followed, and leaned on the fence.

"Quite a view," Hongi said loudly. "What's up?" he asked, from his scarcely moving lips.

"Quite a view," Lan repeated as loudly. "That blue car," he muttered, and stopped. His grey eyes ranged keenly over the wide stretch of ocean, and down the steep cliffs to the wharves below.

They were joined almost immediately by a large man wearing a navy-blue uniform.

"What a day! What a day!" he mopped his forehead.

Hongi smiled briefly.

In the silence of the summer afternoon came the clanking, grinding roar of the dredge, as it cleared the harbour floor. Beyond the marking buoys a tanker seemed to pause, then moved with the slow deliberation of a snail crossing a concrete path. The pilot boat went out to meet the tanker.

"It's got the importance of a chicken guiding a huge and self-important hen," Hongi chuckled.

"Seems strange to be watching ships," the man said. "Usually I'm on them. Work on the *Golden Star*, you know."

"Oh, do you?" Lan showed marked surprise. "It's that one down there, isn't it?"

"Yes, that's it. Quite a sight watching ships come in." The stranger mopped his forehead again.

Lan's grey eyes slid to the navy trousers and highly polished black shoes beside him, and then hastily followed the ship as it came round the third buoy. Its engines moved very slowly. People were hurrying along the wharf. The smoke from the dredge made dark writing in the sky. The little pilot boat towed a thin line from the ship, and then a thick line fastened to it.

"The men on the wharf have caught the thin line," said Lan. He seemed engrossed in the spectacle.

A truck took over the pulling, and the following heavy line was fastened to a bollard. The pilot boat circled, and approaching again, pushed the bow of the ship in towards the wharf. Lan laughed suddenly, "There's the busy little chick of a pilot boat pushing at the huge mother-hen ship." He thought: those ships are in full view of Bluff Hill.

The man in navy moved, as if about to return to the

car, and then paused. "Do you boys come up here often?"
he asked, suddenly.

"Not—not very often," Hongi said, cautiously.

Astern of the ship, the water, churned by the screws,
bloomed muddy in the green-blue of the harbour. In
the bows the winch took up the cable, and slowly pulled
the vessel against the wharf. There was a loud creak as
the ship swung out. From there another cable was attached to a bollard.

The man in navy leaned on the fence, staring at the
ships. He seemed to have forgotten the boys.

The sea lay still as a lake of greenstone, flawed with
churned-up mud. Overhead, two seagulls dipped and
called.

"So that's the course ships take when they come in,"
Lan said, thoughtfully.

The boys turned away, as if by an unspoken consent,
and walked slowly past the blue car. The door had been
left open, and a raincoat was lying across the back seat,
while on the floor lay a metal lamp, with its lens set
inside a short metal barrel.

"Crikey!" Hongi exclaimed, softly.

He strolled over to the fence again, but away from the
man in navy. He stared fixedly at the wharves, and at the
ships at anchor. His eyes narrowed as he studied the
course taken by the tanker as it came into harbour.

"It's time to get cracking," Hongi said, loudly. Together the boys strolled across the grass, and started off
down the road. "Did you see that lamp?" he asked. "I
just wonder what that's used for."

"I'm not sure. I feel it should ring a bell, somewhere—"

"Look!" Hongi, resuming his poker-mask, spoke with

scarcely moving lips. Before them, parked on the side of the road, stood the Rolls-Noise. Licence number 131313. There was no sign of Uncle Bob.

With an outward show of complete indifference, the boys sauntered past it, and when they were round the bend in the road, broke into a steady run. In a few minutes the Rolls-Noise passed them, with Uncle Bob, seemingly quite oblivious of their presence, at the wheel. Beside him, absorbed in watching the scenery, sat Thomas-ina.

"Let's get home as quickly as we can," Lan panted, "and compare notes. We'd better make a map of the wharves, too."

The steady hum of another car engine came nearer and nearer.

"You boys in a hurry?" The blue car drew up beside them.

"Er—no," Hongi backed away.

"We haven't far to go," Lan gasped. "We're training —for the school sports," he added. "Thank you all the same."

"All right," the large man in navy grunted, and the car slid forward.

"Now I'll have to justify that lie by going in for every-thing at the school sports," Lan grinned.

"Hallo, boys," Aunt Jenny called from the front door. She stood neat and plump, smiling contentedly, in the doorway. "I made some ice cream, and I haven't anyone to sample it." She moved aside hastily as what seemed like a tornado passed her.

"Whoops," Hongi said, with his mouth full. "You wouldn't believe that anyone could make ice cream like this. The huge pieces of strawberry—" His lips smacked in appreciation.

"Have some more, Hongi," Aunt Jenny laughed, and gave the grinning Lan some more, too.

"A Mr. Bulke came to see Uncle Bob this afternoon, but he was out with Thomasina, keeping an unobtrusive eye on you," Aunt Jenny said, as she washed the ice cream dishes a few minutes later.

"That was the man in the blue car, wasn't it? The man who whizzed past us when we were coming from the airport?" Lan picked up two dishes, and began to wipe them.

"That's the one." Aunt Jenny finished the dishes. "Sis and Bruffie were at their best, and we were accompanied by howls of rage, because Bruffie had left on the bathroom tap, and the bath had overflowed, and Sis tried to swim in it. Bruffie shouted at the top of his voice that he hadn't had a fair share of the swimming. Then they both turned on their aunt, because she pulled out the plug, and let out the water."

Lan laughed shortly. "And I suppose Mr. Bulke arrived in the middle of all this?"

Aunt Jenny nodded. "Yes, complete with full uniform. It seems that he's quite disturbed because the good name of the *Golden Star* is under a cloud of rumour and suspicion. He told me all about it, as Uncle Bob wasn't here. He was so perturbed that he came to see Uncle Bob, when he was off duty, to ask just what was going on in the customs office, and had they any grounds for suspicion. He even offered to let me search the ship for diamonds!"

Hongi rubbed his sandal against his ankle. "And are you going?" he grinned.

"I am not. But Mr. Bulke was very jolly and friendly, and threw sticks for Wuffit to fetch." Aunt Jenny wiped down the bench. "He got so hot throwing sticks for Wuffit, that he took off his coat and threw it on the lawn. A pocket watch rolled out."

"Oh?" Lan's eyebrows went up.

"Mr. Bulke laughed, and said, 'I always carry two watches. Have to be exactly on time in my job, you know.' I think he meant it all as a joke," Aunt Jenny smiled, "because I noticed the watch wasn't going. Mr. Bulke left soon after that, but he did say he'd probably see us again."

"We'd better write up our notes at headquarters, Senior Detective Lan," Hongi suggested. "We've quite a lot to discuss, as well as sketching a map." They wandered thoughtfully towards the shed, but Lan reappeared in a few minutes.

"Please may we have a lemon or an onion?" he asked Aunt Jenny.

Aunt Jenny regarded him with mock horror. "Have you both got colds this scorching weather? Or are you going to have a competition to see who can eat a raw onion or a lemon first?"

"Neither," Lan gurgled, with a sudden burst of laughter. "It's just that—" he hesitated.

Aunt Jenny smiled. "It's a secret? Well, here's an onion, and a knife to cut it. Dinner will be ready in half an hour, so don't let it ruin your appetite! If you come back smelling strongly of onion, I'll—I'll—send you over to live with Sis and Bruffie!"

"Oh, no, not that! Whatever you do to me, not that, Brer Fox," Lan laughed, and ran off to the shed.

"I can't make it all out," said Hongi as he watched milky drops forming on the cut-up onion.

"I can't either. That Mr. Bulke is a real mystery."

"Perhaps he's playing a double game. Full of goodwill and kind to animals on the surface, but underneath—"

"You could be right." Lan's fingertips beat together rhythmically as he thought.

"And that sailor. He did ask us to look over the *Golden Star*. Are you game to do it?"

"That depends," Lan's fingertips hesitated in their beat, "on whether the captain's on board."

"Yes, I'm not exactly scared of the captain," Hongi admitted, "but I certainly wouldn't like to get in his way."

"Well, I'm frightened of him," Lan said, briefly. "If he's in a diamond smuggling racket it'll mean he's raking in thousands of pounds, or it wouldn't be worthwhile. And anyone who—who didn't exactly help— would have to be wiped out pretty quickly."

"I never thought of that," Hongi said slowly. "It's bigger than I ever dreamed of. Somehow you don't think of crime in a big way in a little town like Napier."

"No," Lan agreed, "you don't. That's why it must seem just made for the job. I'm sure they've got it all thought out, and rehearsed."

"And what we know may lead up a blind alley. We've got to fit in every piece in the jigsaw of the problem."

"Yes, it's quite a jigsaw. Only the pieces might seem to be the right shape, and yet be there only to fool us. Is that what you mean, Senior Detective Hongi?"

"Too right, Senior Detective Lan."

They wrote steadily, first in ink, and then, on fresh paper, in onion juice.

"I hope the Napier heat won't show up this invisible ink," Lan muttered.

"I'll do the map of the wharves and of Bluff Hill, if you like," Hongi offered.

"All right," Lan agreed, as he wrote steadily.

The air was still, warm and scented. The spiders on the windows watched patiently for flies that never seemed to come, and survived in spite of it.

"There's something about that lamp on the seat of the car. Why a lamp like that? Why, Hongi, why?"

"Beats me." Hongi stretched, yawning, and quickly as lightning tipped Lan off his apple box.

"You—!" shouted Lan, as words failed him.

For a full minute they wrestled and fought, twisted and dodged in the joyous abandon of a fun fight.

As suddenly as it had begun the skirmish ended. Hongi dusted down his clothes by slapping them vigorously, and Lan straightened his apple box as carefully as if it had been a fraction out of place.

They wrote steadily until they heard Aunt Jenny calling, "Dinner's ready!"

When Senior Detectives Hongi and Lan emerged from the Headquarters of the Junior C.I.B., the Rolls-Noise was resting on the lawn. Thomasina was not in sight, but Uncle Bob was talking earnestly to Aunt Jenny.

"It's time I went home, Mrs. Sherwood," Hongi smiled. "We've had a wonderful day."

"It isn't over yet," Uncle Bob said. "You haven't forgotten the Mardi Gras to-night, have you?"

"I'll dance a haka!" Hongi grinned with pleasure. "And I'll stay at home all to-morrow and help Mum, just to make up for being out all to-day." He hopped towards the gate, with feet moving as if they were keeping time to some unheard but compelling music.

"What's a haka?" Lan turned to his uncle.

"It's a Maori dance, sometimes a war dance, but Hongi just meant he was pretty pleased." Uncle Bob knocked out his pipe on the nearest fence post. "There's a letter from London for you, Lan. I left it on your bed this morning, but I forgot to tell you about it. The writing on the envelope is your mother's. We sent her a cable when you arrived to say you were safe and well."

For a moment Lan felt a wave of homesickness engulf him. But his father and mother would be coming to New Zealand soon. Somehow it wouldn't be completely like home until they came.

A few minutes later Lan appeared from his bedroom.

"Yes, it's from Mother," he said. "How am I liking New Zealand, and she hopes I am happy and good. But there's a funny bit here. She saw in a newspaper the other day that diamonds are being smuggled overseas to ports of call in the Commonwealth. Wouldn't it be strange, she adds, if we came across this smuggling in New Zealand?"

"Little does she know," Uncle Bob said, darkly, "that she's hit the nail fair and square on the head."

CHAPTER SIX

"But we didn't know the shoe-polish would go all over our clothes, did we, Bruffie?"

"Of course we didn't. We just thought we'd polish all the shoes for a surprise. You should be grateful, Auntie. We're never appreciated, are we, Sis?" His voice rose to a high, metallic whine.

"Well, we'll forget about the red, and the brown and the black shoe polish all over your clothes," their aunt's quiet voice came, wearily. "Though I'm sure I'll never clean it off. Now, share your toys, and see if you can enjoy life for a change. It's wasting your holiday to quarrel every day."

"We *do* enjoy our holiday!"

"Well, I don't. I've never known anything like it." Their aunt's voice had a note of dull despair.

"O-aw--ow! He hit me!"

"It was an accident! It was an accident!" Bruffie shouted, indignantly.

"If I hit you," his aunt's voice was quiet, almost contemplative, "would that be an accident?"

"Oh, no," Bruffie sounded shocked at such a preposterous idea. "That wouldn't be fair. That would be on purpose!"

Uncle Bob put down his pipe with a sudden thud.

"Why do we hear all their rows so clearly?" he asked, savagely.

"They always seem to have them in the same place," Hongi said. "It's a little shelter under a grape-vine near the fence. I've often played in that garden—but never when Sis and Bruffie were there!" he added, grinning, and rubbing one sandalled foot against the other.

"Hm-m," Uncle Bob looked thoughtful. "If we wait a while before we go to the Mardi Gras, the lights will be on—trees like a line of enormous Christmas trees, all lit up. And anyhow, I have a little job to do before we set out." His eyes gleamed, and he knocked out his pipe with sudden, jerky taps. "Just a little matter of a tape-recorder, boys." The boys looked mystified, but Aunt Jenny gave a sudden peal of laughter. Outside, the voices came over the fence in a crescendo of rage.

Later, when they reached the town, after a hiccupping, clanking drive in the Rolls-Noise, they saw the line of high trees along Marine Parade, and every one, like a child's dream of outsize Christmas trees, glowed and twinkled with coloured lights.

"Let's look at Pania," Aunt Jenny suggested.

They stopped by the life-size statue of Pania of the Reef, and Hongi read them the words set into the base of the statue, which told the Maori legend of how Pania was lured by the siren voices of the sea people, and swam out to meet them. She wanted to return, but was changed into the reef beyond Napier breakwater.

They stood then and watched the wraith-like mystery of the changing shapes and colours of the Parker fountain, and paused in silence by the Perpetual Light of Memory.

"We'd better keep together, boys," Uncle Bob said, rounding up Hongi and Lan, who were gazing at the sea, and talking in low tones. "It'll be getting crowded, and we're going back to the side-shows."

From the showground came the sound of music, loud, insistent, with the throbbing rhythm that seems to be part of the lure of fairs and shows all the world over.

"Wonder if we'll hear that tune, Lan?" Hongi said softly.

"'The Roundabout'? I'm keeping my ears peeled. It might be a clue. None of the outfits along there are playing it, anyway. I half expected the merry-go-rounds to have it."

"I had a bit of a notion like that, myself," said Hongi who seemed to be listening.

"If we see any of the men from the *Golden Star* we'd better keep just behind Uncle Bob, as if we didn't know him," Lan said, softly.

The crowd was increasing, and with others they stopped for a while to watch the skaters gliding, turning, and making figures on the skating rink. The skating changed to waltz time, and they watched, mesmerised by the lights and the gliding, rhythmic movements.

They crossed through the car park to the blaring music, the big wheel, the darts, the games of skill, the stalls and the merry-go-rounds.

"I want that one!" Loud and shrill came the demanding cry, in a voice that seemed all too familiar.

"Sis and Bruffie, themselves and in person," Hongi grinned. "I've seen them before. There they are with their aunt, Miss Johnson, near that stall selling statuettes of Pania of the Reef."

Lan looked, but the milling crowd hid them from view.

"Sis and Bruffie?" Uncle Bob's head jerked round. "I want a word in private with their aunt." He turned to Aunt Jenny. "That is, unless you'd like to put the proposition up to Miss Johnson yourself?"

"No, I'll look after the children, and leave you to it," Aunt Jenny smiled at him, as if they shared some secret joke. Laughing, Uncle Bob crossed to a rather harrassed looking woman, holding a little girl's hand.

With a swift wrench the child twisted away, and shrilled again: "I want that one!"

Hongi and Lan moved closer. The twins were looking at the stall of Pania statuettes. Curly-haired, fair, blue-eyed, chubby, they looked as if they had stepped out from the leaves of the more uplifting type of story-book. The impression remained until their shrill voices rent the air.

"We-ell," breathed Lan, "I'm quite bowled over! I thought they'd look like something the cat brought in."

The boys, watching, saw Miss Johnson pay for two statuettes, and hand them to the twins. As Uncle Bob approached, Sis screamed for the third time, "Want that one!" She watched Uncle Bob in silence as he spoke to her aunt, and as they turned aside, deep in conversation, Hongi and Lan saw her quickly reach to the back of the stall, put back her Pania statuette, and change it for the one of her choice. It was so swiftly done, that neither her aunt nor the man in charge of the stall, who had turned aside for a moment, noticed anything.

In complete silence, in an attitude of somewhat prim obedience, the twins re-joined their aunt as Uncle Bob was taking his leave of her. Miss Johnson gave a sudden burst of laughter, in which Uncle Bob joined, and waved to Aunt Jenny, who was laughing heartily herself.

"It's a secret," she explained to Hongi and Lan. "You'll know all about it when we've worked it out properly in a few days' time."

"It ought to be good," Hongi grinned, rubbing his right toe on his left ankle.

"It ought to fix Sis and Bruffie," Uncle Bob said with evident satisfaction.

"I suppose you boys are too old for Panias?" Uncle Bob asked Hongi and Lan.

"Too right," grinned Hongi, "but I'd like to have a look at one."

"I'll buy one to send to Mother," said Lan crossing to the stall. He held his purchase out to Hongi.

"My word, it's heavy. Like lead." Hongi weighed it in his hand, and passed it back to Lan.

It was then that Lan heard it. At first he thought he had imagined those notes, so faintly were they whistled, then very slightly louder he heard them. 'The Rounda-bout'. His fingers gripped Hongi's wrist and tightened on it in warning. Slowly they turned.

If they expected to see sailors from the *Golden Star* they were disappointed. In the milling throng it was difficult to decide where the whistle had come from.

"Come on, dear," a woman hurried a child on to the merry-go-round before the music started again, and the merry-go-round moved slowly, and then gathered speed.

A youth, whistling a catchy tune, danced past, his feet marking their course in the tiny pebbles on the

ground, clearing the cigarette packets, the drinking-
straws, the pieces of paper, ice cream cartons and a dropped handkerchief.

A family group, chattering and laughing, crowded
round a stall, and tried their skill at knocking down a
grinning Uncle Remus. A man, thin, rat-like, leaned over
the Pania stall. He bought a statuette, and the stall
keeper wrapped it up, and passed it over to him.

"Can't see a thing," Hongi shrugged, and turned his
hands palms upwards. Lan shrugged in reply. They
followed Uncle Bob. In the blare of the music, the jost-
ling throng, the heady excitement of the Mardi Gras, the
fun and the laughter, they forgot the haunting notes of
the song, and the tantalising puzzles of diamonds and
smuggling.

Lights twinkled in the trees, and shone from the big
wheel and the stalls; the crowd of Maori and pakeha
pushed, jostled and talked loudly and eagerly. Ornaments,
brightly painted vases, clocks and glittering necklaces
gave colour to the stalls.

"Look what I've won!" a voice would shout, and
occasionally, one of these ornaments would be carried
triumphantly away. Music blared, different tunes clashed
like discordant cymbals, and voices were raised in laughter
and earnestness. Above all came the smells of the fair—
the sweetness of ice cream and chocolate, the pungent
odour of dust and heat and crowds.

"Let's have a go at the dodgems," Hongi called.

He and Lan rode on the dodgem cars, twisting, bump-
ing and turning.

"It's time we went home," Uncle Bob said, at last, after
they had all paddled in the double boats on the artificial

lake. They walked under the lighted Christmas trees to the waiting Rolls-Noise.

"To-night we'd better note down anything that might be a clue, Senior Detective Hongi," Lan said, quietly.

"A clue?" asked Aunt Jenny. "I'm all agog. What mystery is this?"

"Nothing much, so far," Lan smiled at her. "We're detectives, and we try to be aware of everything, every sight, sound, smell, touch and things like that. And perhaps, when it's all added up, we might find out something."

"You might, at that," Aunt Jenny encouraged. "It'll make life a lot more interesting, anyway."

They crowded into the Rolls-Noise, and the car coughed, spluttered, and finally started, with a jerk and a rush.

"It really was bonzer, eh?" Hongi breathed, happily. "Thank you very much, indeed," he added, politely, his lips parting in a delighted grin.

"It was super-duper, all right," Lan agreed. "Thanks a lot, Uncle and Aunt."

"We sort of enjoyed it ourselves," Aunt Jenny said softly.

"That tune," Hongi frowned.

"I heard it, too," Lan said, "but I couldn't see a single thing that might give us a clue."

They drove in silence under the lighted archways of the city, and in low voices admired the decorated buildings and lights. They stopped at Hongi's gate.

"Good night! Good night!"

"Thanks a lot!"

As they drove through their own front gate, the silence

of the night and the asthmatic cough of the Rolls-Noise were broken by the shrill voices of Sis and Bruffie.

"She won't let me touch her Pania!"

"I will, too. Take that, Bruffie! And that!"

"O-oh! She threw it at me! It's gone right over the fence. Serves you right!"

Miss Johnson's voice, unexpectedly firm, replied:

"You deliberately threw the Pania statuette. Well, it'll stay there for to-night. Come inside, at once, both of you!"

When the car stopped Aunt Jenny turned to Lan.

"Don't bother looking for their Pania statuette to-night. Just have a bath, and then off to bed. It's quite late."

Lan smiled, smelling the clear, fresh smells of the night as he stepped from the car, and nodded agreement.

"It's been super. Just super-duper," Lan breathed happily.

CHAPTER SEVEN

"I'VE DONE a bit of snooping," Uncle Bob announced the next day. "Remember that blue car, the one Mr. Bulke from the *Golden Star* was driving? Well, he had a perfect right to it. I found out that its owner is away for a few days, and let Bulke have it while his ship's in Napier."

"Oh," Lan looked up. "Was that why the Rolls-Noise was parked near Bluff Hill? While you did your snooping, I mean?"

"Sort of," Uncle Bob admitted slowly, filling his pipe, and pulling on it with deep concentration until it began to draw. "I was also snooping then about something different. Keeping an eye on you and Hongi." Then abruptly, "Ever seen an Aldis lamp, Lan?" Without waiting for a reply he went on, "You could signal from Bluff Hill to a ship without anyone being much wiser. That is, you could if you had the right kind of signalling lamp, and had everything arranged beforehand. You'd know then, just what place to signal to."

"You mean that I could signal to you on a ship if I told you to stand exactly at the foot of the mast, for instance?" Lan asked.

"Yes, with certain signals you could—and with a hooded beam no one would get that signal but me. At any rate, over a short distance."

66

"Hm-m," Lan seemed deep in thought. "Gosh!" Lan stood up as if in a dream. "Gee!" a sudden thought seemed to have struck him. "I think I'll ring up Hongi, and see if he can come fishing from the wharf. That is, if you and Aunt Jenny don't want us for anything."

His uncle crossed to the window, opened it, and called, "Do you want Lan for anything this morning, Jenny?"

From the direction of the clothes-line Aunt Jenny replied, "No, I'm going into town to get a cool dress." She opened the back door and came into the kitchen. "Did you know that it's ninety in the shade?"

"Wow!" Lan grinned. "So that's why I feel as if I'd been put through the wringer? I thought I'd get hold of Hongi, and go fishing from the wharf if it's all right with you."

"That would be fine," said Aunt Jenny as she pushed back a strand of hair with the back of her hand. "You could take Wuffit, and give him a run. He's just in the mood to go noising and nosing about, even though it's so hot." She moved towards the kitchen. "You ring Hongi, and then come and tell me what boys like for lunch."

"Hongi says it'd be super-duper and scrummy," Lan said when he returned from the telephone, and dropped on to a chair in the kitchen. He buttered bread lavishly, added peanut butter and creamed honey, and slammed down another piece of bread on top. Absent-mindedly he ate the sandwich.

Aunt Jenny's eyes twinkled. "No," she said as Lan was about to devour the second sandwich. "You've just had breakfast. This is for lunch. Remember?"

Lan laughed sheepishly. "Well, of all the things! I was wondering where that sandwich had disappeared to!"

"Ah, here's Hongi now. It didn't take him much time to—"

"I just zipped along," Hongi grinned as he opened the screen door. He sat down and helped with the lunch.

"That's a nice Pania statuette, Lan."

"Uncle's going to post it to Mom," Lan handed it to Hongi.

Hongi grinned, ran a brown finger down the smooth side of the Pania statuette, and sang:

"'Hoea Mai te Waka'. It's not a cradle song," he explained. "It's actually 'Paddle the Canoe', but I doubt if Pania would mind."

Aunt Jenny turned towards the table. "Here are peaches, apricots and apples. Oh, and tomatoes, too, and a real grapefruit drink."

"Oh, scrummy. Really scrummy!" Hongi's eyes gleamed.

"You know," Lan said, slowly, "I just wouldn't have believed all this in London. Lashings of fruit, and ninety in the shade. And, what's funniest of all, I'm behaving as if I were accustomed to this all my life." He sniffed the sweet smell of the apples, and held a tomato up to the light, his eyes drinking in its rich colour.

"It's the different food smells, and the smell of Uncle's pipe, and the feeling of grass under your bare feet, and crisp, cold lettuce, and the big, gliding butterflies—"

"And the insects," Hongi added, enthusiastically. "I got a praying mantis for my collection this morning. It's such a pious-looking thing, just resting there as if it

were praying. But just let a fly come near and the praying
mantis grabs it and gobbles it up alive. Preying, not
praying!"

"Ugh!" Aunt Jenny made a face at him.

"Uncle Bob should hear that one. He goes for puns in
a big way," Lan grinned. "Before I forget—one of the
terrible twins biffed a Pania statuette over here last night.
Did they find it?"

"No, I don't think they looked," Aunt Jenny wrinkled
her forehead. "I suppose they forgot all about it. I'd
forgotten it myself."

When they left Lan was carrying the lunch in a knapsack, and Hongi the fishing rod, the bait, and some
chocolate. At their feet, between their legs, in front and
behind them, gambolled Wuffit. His tongue hung out, and
his mouth was open in a wide smile of panting enjoyment.
The metallic song of an unseen cicada rasped on the summer air.

"Crayfish and cannonballs," Hongi said, contentedly,
striding beside Lan. "This is the life."

A large bird, disturbed by their footsteps, flew up off the
ground. Lan gazed at its dark head and the large splotch
of white on each wing.

"I haven't seen one of those before," he said.

"Oh, lots of those about," said Hongi glancing at the
bird. "They're minahs. We had a pet one once, that could
talk."

They could smell the sea now, although they were
not yet in sight of it. Unconsciously they hurried.

"Any more clues, Senior Detective Lan?" Hongi asked.

"I don't know," Lan's steps slowed down. "I'm trying
to keep everything in mind. And I'm trying to follow

up everything. Gosh, you have to be alert! I've written out a full report of everything I know. It's locked safely in the headquarters shed."

"I've written out everything I could think of, too." Hongi swiped at a plantain head. "Is this fishing idea business or pleasure, Senior Detective Lan?"

"Well, Senior Detective Hongi," Lan laughed, "with Wuffit along it could be anything. If you don't get out from between my legs while I'm trying to walk, Wuffit Sherwood, I'll—I'll—" Words failed him.

"Here, fetch it, Wuffit!" Hongi threw a stick along the ground. With a flurry of long hair, a wild scampering, and a sharp braking of skidding claws, Wuffit chased the stick, caught it in the air, and bore it in triumph to Hongi.

Lan slipped a lead on to Wuffit's collar. "Steady, old boy," he said, quietly. "We're going to cross Marine Parade. You steady down." Wuffit immediately took on the air of a poodle parading in a circus. Then, with high, almost mincing steps, he advanced in the manner of a dog of fashion taking his mistress for a stroll along a street in Paris.

Hongi roared with laughter. "Here, you bucket-brained pup, no putting on the dog with us!"

Lan laughed, too, and Wuffit, scenting a frolic, forgot how fashionable he was and scampered along gaily, pulling Lan after him.

The wharf was almost empty. There were a few boys fishing over the far end, but no one fished near the *Golden Star*.

"They'll begin to wonder why we fish here," Hongi remarked, quietly. "Perhaps we'd better eat this choco-late before it melts. I don't think it'll last much longer."

"Well, of course not," Lan grinned, "especially if we eat it."

Hongi clenched his fist, grinned broadly, and aimed a sharp uppercut at Lan's jaw. It deliberately stopped two inches short. "Corker chocolate." He broke off two more pieces. "Want some, Wuffit?" He unleashed him.

Wuffit barked once, sharply, in reply. He snapped at, and ate his piece of melting chocolate as if it were full of bones.

"It won't break your teeth, Wuffit," Lan laughed.

"Hey, you boys!" a cheerful voice hailed them from the deck of the *Golden Star*. They looked up and saw the seaman they had rescued. "Like to see over the ship?"

"Too right, we would," Hongi shouted back, and shouldered the knapsack.

"Thank you very much," Lan called, politely.

"Wuff! Wuff!" Wuffit scampered up the gangway before the boys had time to collect their gear.

"Keep your eyes skinned, Hongi," Lan's lips scarcely moved.

"Too right," Hongi's face was expressionless.

"My name's Puddick," the seaman greeted them. "You the boys that pulled me out of the water, and got me breathing again?" They nodded. "Thought so. Got a bit of a present for you both in my cabin. Always liked to look over a ship myself, when I was a lad." The seaman, with twinkling blue eyes, stood for a moment at the top of the gangway. He rubbed his hand through his thinning brown hair, and laughed loudly.

"Wondered what had struck me when that dog of yours came charging between my legs. Bit of a flurry he was in, too." He swayed, off balance, and sat down suddenly.

"Well, of all the—"

Wuffit earnestly, and with dignity, crawled out from the seaman's feet, stood on his own hind legs, and held out one paw. Lan dived at him, caught him, and with what seemed like a single movement, slipped the lead on to Wuffit's collar. Wuffit promptly did his French-poodle-mincing-on-parade act. Mr. Puddick roared with laughter as he staggered to his feet.

"Don't suppose you'd like to give him to me? He'd be just the thing for a ship's pet."

"Oh, no," Lan shook his head, decidedly. "We want him ourselves."

"Thought you would," Mr. Puddick laughed.

"Come along and see the ship. Can't thank you enough for saving me the other day. Guess I'm just another seaman who can't swim. But I'm jolly well going to learn. You can bet your life on that." He moved across the deck, and the boys and Wuffit followed.

The ship was newly scrubbed, the paintwork gleamed. The dining room sported futuristic fish on wall murals and chromium-framed tables and chairs. The lounge drew a gasp of admiration from Lan.

"It's super, isn't it? All those beautiful woods, and the rich, coloured drapes, like ripe tomatoes." He held Wuffit firmly by the collar.

"Cost a pretty penny," the seaman agreed. "I don't see much of this part of the ship, but the old man and most of the big brass are away to-day, so I thought I'd like to have a look-see again, and watch your eyes pop out at the same time." Laughing, he turned to go. Hongi followed.

I must keep my eyes open, Lan thought. You never know what will turn up. Every nook and cranny. Every possible hiding place.

His eyes skimmed over chromium fittings, mentally removing them, hiding diamonds behind them and replacing them. How much was possible? How much was probable? Yet somewhere on this ship he was convinced there lurked a hiding place. His eyes hardened like steel as they roved everywhere.

The ship smell of food and paint and oil lingered in the passages, as Lan, holding tightly on to Wuffit's lead, followed Hongi and Mr. Puddick.

"Here, Wuffit, stop tying me up with that lead." He untwisted himself, as Wuffit, delighted with this new experience, ran in frenzied circles round him.

"Rare dog, that," Mr. Puddick paused, laughing. "Knows what he's doing, too. I'd like to let him loose on the old man sometime, just for a bit of a lark. Just wouldn't we see the sparks fly!"

"He's very well-behaved, sometimes," Lan said earnestly.

"Yes, sometimes," Hongi grinned. "It's that 'some-times' that's the catch. Usually you just don't know what he'll do."

"No, but I could guess!" roared Mr. Puddick in a loud burst of laughter.

With a sudden twist Wuffit tore away from Lan's grasp, dashed past Hongi, and between the seaman's legs.

Mr. Puddick staggered, caught at a chair, and steadied himself before he fell. Lan, with a muttered apology, tore after Wuffit.

Down passageways they rushed, through doorways,

up stairs, into cabins, under beds and away down long passages again. Sometimes Lan drew near enough to hear Wuffit's claws scraping on the floor, before he was off again at what seemed to be the speed of light.

There was a great and sudden calm, broken by a single "Wuff!" In a cabin, under a bunk, Wuffit was sniffing noisily. He came out quietly, and as Lan pounced upon him, and grasped his lead, Wuffit dropped what he had in his mouth. Lan picked up the big, old-fashioned watch, strangely light in weight.

As if released by some secret spring the back flew open. There were no works inside. Nothing at all, just an empty, gold watch case, with a few deep scratches inside on the gold.

CHAPTER EIGHT

THE SILENT WATCH

THERE WERE footsteps approaching.

"Lan, did you catch him?" Hongi called.

Questions crowded into Lan's mind. Was this Mr. Bulke's cabin? Was this the watch Aunt Jenny saw? The one that wasn't going? The one Mr. Bulke said he needed as a check on his other watch to make sure he was on time? If it is, he won't want anyone to see it, Lan thought. With his foot he pushed it quickly behind a box under the bunk, grasped Wuffit's collar firmly, and answered.

"Here, Hongi. I've got him safe and sound." He pulled Wuffit as he tried again to search out the watch case. As the seaman and Hongi reached the door Lan stepped from the cabin. Hongi, watching, saw a cold mask of politeness hide Lan's excitement.

"Gosh, that was a chase," Lan grinned. Casually he asked, "Whose cabin did he land up in?"

"Oh, this is old Bulke's cubby-hole. He'd be pretty sore if he knew a dog had been nosing round it. Very fussy he is about his cabin. Very fussy indeed." Mr. Puddick laughed, showing a gap in his front teeth.

"Thank you very much," Lan smiled, politely. "It was wonderful seeing over the ship."

"Really corker," Hongi grinned, his teeth very white against his brown skin, "but I think we'd better get a move on, now. I don't like to think what Wuffit will get into next."

"Quite a lot of things, I'll be bound," the seaman laughed. "Well, it was nice having you boys, and seeing your eyes pop out when you saw them fancy woods in the lounge."

With a sudden bound Wuffit started racing. Round and round Lan he circled, with Lan grimly holding on to the leash. Then as a final effort he made for the boy's legs. Lan sat down, heavily.

Hongi, shaking with silent laughter, unwound the leash.

"Bad dog," he scolded. Wuffit slunk under Mr. Bulke's bunk, and with drooping ears peeped out, with eager, lolling tongue.

Lan scrambled hastily to his feet. With anxious haste he grasped Wuffit by the collar, and slid him out.

"You're not going on fishing there, are you?" Mr. Puddick asked, as they reached the deck. "It's much better farther along the wharf."

"No," Hongi answered. "We might go for a tramp somewhere."

Unthinking, Lan glanced up at Bluff Hill. The seaman followed his eyes.

"There's a good walk up there, I believe, and quite a view at the end of it. But wait a minute, just before you go—" He hurried away, and soon reappeared bearing two of the largest boxes of chocolates the boys had ever seen. "And there's a couple of adventure books for you, too. All about ships they are. You'll enjoy reading them."

"Aw gee!" Hongi protested. "We didn't expect all this. But thanks—thanks a lot!"

"They're smashing. Really smashing. You certainly know what boys like, Mr. Puddick." Lan smiled his thanks as they packed the chocolates and the books into the knapsack.

"'Course I know what boys like," the seaman replied. "Got two boys of my own in London. Well, so long for now. It's a grand day for Bluff Hill."

"We might walk up there then," Hongi agreed, and they thanked the man again, and steering Wuffit carefully, they left the ship.

"I think," Lan said, with unmoving lips, as they stepped on to the wharf, "that we'd better make ourselves scarce." Aloud he said, "Wasn't it jolly nice to see over that ship?"

"Oh, supersonic!" Hongi agreed loudly.

They strolled down the wharf. Wuffit minced beside them.

"Well, Senior Detective Lan?"

They spoke in low tones, earnestly.

"I looked everywhere I could think of, Senior Detective Hongi."

"So did I, Senior Detective Lan. But I didn't get much further. I suppose the customs people are up to all the tricks. We're two silly coots, really, if we think we can do better than they can, after all their years at the game."

"Yes," Lan agreed, his fingers lacing and interlacing. "Yet, I don't know. Sometimes you don't realise what something is like even if you see it every day of your life. For instance, have our kitchen chairs got spokes at the back?"

"Yes, they have. But what on earth—?"

"All right, but how many spokes has each chair?"

"Four," Hongi said promptly, "or five. I couldn't be sure. I think I see what you mean, now. People see things without being aware of them, is that it?"

"That's it," Lan agreed.

"And anyway, how many spokes have those chairs? Or don't you know?" Hongi teased him.

"'Course I know, or I wouldn't show up my ignorance by asking you. Four of the chairs have five bars down the back and three underneath, but the fifth has four bars down the back and four supporting the legs underneath. I see them every day."

"And you realise what you're seeing," Hongi said, slowly.

"When we were on the ship, I looked particularly at taps and things like that, in case they could be unscrewed, and the loot hidden in there," Lan said thoughtfully, pursing his lips and frowning. "But I couldn't find out much about them without unscrewing them, and that was impossible with Mr. Puddick in close attendance."

"I noticed that some but not all of the cupboard doors seemed to be made of plywood, so I suppose they're hollow inside," Hongi said. "Or if it's not plywood you could scoop out secret hidey holes on top without anyone being any the wiser."

"Or you could put the diamonds in a bag, and fasten it or nail it, so that it fell into position in the hollow door, but was secure against falling down to the bottom." Hongi's steps slowed as he pondered. "I thought of pipes, too. Drain pipes." Hongi plucked off a piece of grass and tore it into small pieces. "You could hide things in the U-bend of a hand basin, if you were jolly careful not to let anyone use the basin for washing."

"It'd take us a hundred years finding the place, because we can't go and rip up things," Lan said, his teeth biting against his bottom lip. "But I did find out something. Or Wuffit did. A watch, Hongi, or rather an empty watch case, covered inside with scratches all over the gold."

They were interrupted by Flying Officer Wuffit, who had seen a cat.

"You rascal pup!" Hongi panted, as, half-way up Coote Road, they finally caught up with Wuffit, trailing his leash.

"Golly, it's hot," said Lan and rubbed the back of his hand over his forehead. "I can't even think clearly. It was ninety in the shade this morning. I wonder what it is now?"

"Probably only about ninety-five."

"'Only about ninety-five,' he says," Lan groaned hollowly.

"I wonder." Hongi scraped his sandals in the dust. "I wonder. An empty watch case, and inside, scratches all over the gold."

The path rose more steeply. Lan looked at the lush growth in the gardens, and the smell of many flowers came to them on the breathless air. Grape fruit and oranges, poppies and petunias, he noted.

The Rolls-Noise stood at the roadside. "Uncle Bob ferreting again," Lan grinned. "The old Rolls-Noise isn't able to go to the top of the hill." They passed the bowling green, and now walked on the right of the winding road. On one side there were chestnut trees, on the other a high, grassy, flower-freckled bank.

"Let's have our lunch in the shade of one of the lookouts," Hongi suggested, as they reached the top of the hill.

Lan nodded, and they dropped down in the shade of the concrete building. Even Flying Officer Wuffit promptly went to sleep, worn out by his busy morning.

They sat gulping in huge draughts of the warm, scented air.

"Not much like the London smog," Lan grinned.

The sea smell mingled with that of the flowers, and the huge dome of sky was very blue above them.

"It doesn't seem real," he added, "and I miss the cockney voices, and the expressions they use there. The woman who lived next door to us used to say, 'Lord love a duck' whenever she was surprised, which was all the time, actually."

"It's real, all right," Hongi laughed, "but it's a bit different from the roar and rush and smell of London, I guess."

"The people here in the streets speak quickly, and have flatter voices. Isn't that it? And you seldom hear 'coo' and 'smashing', for instance. But you hear 'she'll be right' and 'fair go'," Lan pondered aloud.

"And 'it's a fair cow' when they don't like anything," Hongi chuckled.

They ate their lunch in the almost breathless silence. A single cicada began to rasp about summer, and then was still. It all seemed as unreal as a painted landscape on a huge canvas—a landscape with unnaturally blue sky, too green grass, and too sharply defined, square concrete buildings.

The dredge in the harbour began its clanking, grinding roar, breaking the silence. Lan wiped some cake crumbs from his mouth, and strolled over to the fence above the cliff, and gazed at the *Golden Star*. Hongi, wrestling juicily with a ripe peach, joined him.

"Well, Senior Detective Lan?"

"What do you think, Senior Detective Hongi?"

Hongi aimed his peach stone, and threw it at a large cactus growing down the face of the cliff.

"I can't be sure of anything. But I've a feeling about the *Golden Star*. I'm as bad as Thomasina with her hunches."

They spoke quietly, although there was no one to overhear.

They strolled back, and sat down by the still-sleeping Wuffit. Above the clanking of the dredge came the sound of a car in low gear mounting nearer and nearer. The noise of the car engine suddenly stopped.

"She's stalled again," a voice growled, angrily.

Lan peeped round the concrete wall. He stiffened, and grasped Hongi's wrist tightly.

"It's Mr. Bulke and Mr. Puddick. Let's keep out of sight. They're trying to get the car started again."

"Can't get her going," the voice muttered angrily. "Looks like we'll have to walk back."

"Wild goose chase, coming up here," the other voice replied, and Lan recognised it as that of Mr. Bulke. "There's not a sign of those two boys. I'll swear one of them got off with that watch. It was in my cabin—"

"I'm sure they didn't take it, sir. Nice boys they are. Saved my life. But I suppose we'd better get the watch business cleared up if we can."

Flying Officer Wuffit awoke, stretched elaborately, and seemed to yawn delicately. He smelled the concrete with care. Then he was off, barking shrilly, pausing and barking again at a single low-flying seagull.

"Let's scram!" Hongi and Lan said, as if with one voice. Hongi picked up the knapsack.

"Leave the fishing things," he said. "We'll get them later."

"That's their dog!" they heard the seaman shout. "They can't be far away."

Hongi and Lan dashed across the grass, whistling to Wuffit, who bounded after them, delighted at the prospect of a new game.

"Here, you boys!" roared Mr. Bulke. "Just as the car broke down," they heard him growl, as he and Mr. Puddick set off in pursuit. "I saw that old crock that Sherwood drives parked down the hill. We could borrow that, if it's still there." Then, raising his voice, "Hey, stop, you two! Stop, I tell you!"

Hongi and Lan, followed by Wuffit, ran the faster.

"We've got to stop him taking the Rolls-Noise," Lan gasped. "Uncle Bob showed me how to take out the rotor, so it wouldn't go."

"I know a short cut down," gasped Hongi, plunging up the bank and into the trees. Lan followed.

"If only we can get to the Rolls-Noise first," he panted.

As they pushed through the bushes they could hear the heavy following footsteps.

"We'll get them yet," grunted Mr. Bulke's deep voice. "They can't keep it up in this heat."

"Neither can you," Hongi muttered.

Little twigs broke under their feet, the smell of mingled flowers wafted gently about them. They leaped and dropped down the steep, bushy bank. The road was before them, dusty, stony. They ran steadily, neck and neck, each spurring the other to greater effort.

"We'll do it," Hongi gasped. "Golly, I've got an awful stitch in my side."

They could hear the pounding footsteps behind them, but their pursuers were hidden by bends in the twisting road. Nearer and nearer. A stone rolled under Lan's foot, and with a sharp cry he skidded and fell heavily.

Hongi stopped, and came back. "Quick, Lan!"

"I—I can't. It's my arm. I came right down on it." He groaned as he tried to move it. "We've got to get the rotor out of the Rolls-Noise. It's the only way to stop them. But gosh, it hurts whenever I jolt it."

With deep, panting gasps they pressed on. The footsteps behind them slowed.

"They're finding the pace too much," Hongi gasped. But the steps started again, running more swiftly this time. Nearer. Nearer.

"There she is! There's the Rolls-Noise," Lan muttered, biting on his lower lip.

"We'll do it. We'll do it yet, "Hongi breathlessly encouraged, doubling up for a second with the pain in his side.

"Golly, the stitch is getting worse," he panted.

"We'll do it," Lan repeated, gasping.

Hongi threw himself on the car and wrenched open the bonnet. Lan reached it, and leaning forward, with Hongi's help, uncovered the distributor, and jerked out the rotor.

Silently he handed it to Hongi. "I can't go on," he muttered.

"Down the bank then!" Hongi whispered urgently.

Lan cradled his left arm with his right hand and dropped from sight in the bushes.

Hongi sped away, as if he had his second wind, and Lan, scarcely daring to breathe, lay listening to the pounding of the approaching footsteps. Wuffit shot off after Hongi, a flurry of furry hair.

"There it is! There's Sherwood's old crock! We'll catch those boys easily. Here! The bonnet's been left open. It wasn't like that when we came up. I'll bet that those boys—It won't start. Here, you crank it. I pride myself that I can get any car going that you like to name," Mr. Bulke's voice came heavily to Lan.

He held his breath. His ears felt as if a tight skin were stretched over them, as he strained to listen. Trickles of sweat poured down his back and his forehead, but Lan did not notice. His arm throbbed, and the slightest movement sent stabs of pain shooting through it. He let his breath go in little outward puffs, careful not to be heard. The sun beat down. The leaves stirred gently. The insect life went on as before. An ant crawled along the hairs on Lan's leg. Impatiently he brushed the tickling insect off. Another followed it.

"Well, what do you know? They've taken the rotor out. The little—! Just let me catch up with them!" Lan could hear the rising anger in Mr. Bulke's voice. He crouched lower, scarcely breathing. A drop of sweat fell from his forehead as he bent forwards. It glistened on a leaf in the sunshine. Lan studied it carefully. More drops followed it. The sun beat down mercilessly.

I don't think I can stand this heat. I'll have to move, Lan thought, desperately. The drops of sweat continued to fall. Lan gasped. His tongue felt dry and thick. His lips had a faint salty taste as he ran his dry tongue over them. He moved cautiously. Jabs of pain arrowed through his arm. Suddenly, "Here's their dog, sir," Mr. Puddick almost shouted in his excitement. "They can't be far away. We'll probably catch up with them all right."

"Is that their dog?" Lan could hear a new note in Mr. Bulke's voice. "I hadn't realised it before, but it's also," he said, triumphantly, "the dog that Sherwood owns. They must be friends or relations. I spent quite a while recently throwing sticks for that dog. Here, Wuffit, good dog! Good dog! So you want me to throw something for you to fetch? Well," Lan could hear the gathering amazement in his voice, "what's that you've got? Well, what do you know? It's the car rotor!"

"Oh, Wuffit," groaned Lan inwardly, "you empty-headed, bucket-brained noodle of a pup."

But Wuffit had not yet finished his work. Lan could hear him sniffing nearer and nearer. With a loud bark of joy he hurled himself down the bank, and, standing firmly with his front paws on Lan's rapidly-swelling sprained arm, barked louder and louder with determined and insistent frenzy.

CHAPTER NINE

WHEN HONGI, grasping the rotor, left Lan hidden by the bank, Wuffit ran along joyously beside him. The sunlight poured down, and Hongi could feel little rivulets of perspiration flowing down his forehead. He gasped, gulping the hot, flower-scented air. He could no longer hear the voices above him, and he paused for a second listening for footsteps. There was silence.

"Come on, Wuffit!" he gasped.

Then, with a growl of joy, Wuffit rushed at Hongi's legs. Caught unawares, Hongi staggered and fell, letting the rotor drop and roll on the road. With a scurry and a scraping of claws Wuffit pounced, mouthed up the rotor, and set back up the hill as fast as his legs would carry him.

With a low moan Hongi watched him go.

"Well," he muttered to himself, "I might as well hurry on and get away before they get the rotor from Wuffit. The best thing to do would be to get Lan's Aunt Jenny, if she's home now, to ring for a taxi for Lan. 'Course he'd be able to get down in time, once those men go, but that arm seemed pretty painful. Oh, Wuffit," he groaned, "why do you have to be such a crazy mutt?"

Hongi ran faster and faster as his way lay down hill. He turned away from the main roads, and hurried along the quieter ones, where he was less likely to be followed.

His side began to ache again with dull throbs, but he

pressed on. Past the Phoenix palms, on and on through the summer heat, panting and gasping. His footsteps slowed, until he heard the cough of a car in the distance.

"The Rolls-Noise," he muttered, wearily. "I haven't a hope if they come this way. I was sure glad to get away from those men. Mr. Bulke would never believe that we didn't take that watch." Hongi ran a dry tongue over his parched lips. They felt thick and corrugated.

He half-ran, half-walked now in the burning sun. A picture of the Sherwood house danced, as tantalising as a mirage, in front of his eyes. His thoughts kept reaching out to it, and his feet seemed clumsy and slow, because they could not fly as swiftly as thoughts. Only two more minutes and he'd be there. Only one minute now.

He stumbled through the gate, his eyes on the ground, wearily. His foot rolled on something, and he tripped, but did not fall. He bent and picked up a statuette of Pania half-hidden in the long grass.

"That'll be the one Sis or Bruffie threw over," he grinned in spite of his weariness. "It feels lighter than the one for Lan's mother."

Suddenly the half-formed smile died on his face. Along the back of his hand blood welled and trickled from a newly-made cut. Hongi stood staring at the statuette, and at the blood.

"Hello, Hongi," Lan's voice said, softly.

Hongi dropped the statuette and gasped, "You, Lan? How on earth did you get here?" He picked up the statuette, and crossed to the porch where his friend was sitting with a bandaged arm supported by a sling made of two large handkerchiefs.

"Well," Lan's grin of pleasure was as wide as Hongi's, "when you left me that darn fool Wuffit came galloping up the road with the rotor—"

"He made straight for my legs, and when I fell and dropped the rotor he made off with it—"

"Yes, I guessed that's what had happened," Lan grinned. "Well, Mr. Bulke had thrown things for Wuffit to fetch, so, of course, Wuffit dropped the rotor at his feet, and waited hopefully for a game. I lay down the bank, sweating, and all but roaring with rage, while Mr. Bulke welcomed Wuffit and recognised the rotor."

"I could drop that pup into a—" Hongi's imagination failed.

"Then, to crown everything, when Wuffit realised that the rotor wasn't going to be thrown for him to fetch, he started sniffing about, and sure enough, guess who he found over the bank!" Lan laughed, bitterly. "He charged down barking loud and insistent welcomes, stood on my ricked elbow, and demanded at the top of his bark that everyone should come and see who was there!"

Hongi shook his fist at an imaginary Wuffit.

"Mr. Puddick came over, and as the game was up I tried to climb the bank. He called out to Mr. Bulke, 'It's the young fellah, who was in your cabin.' At that moment came an icy voice, 'And what are you doing with this car?'"

"Your Uncle Bob?" asked Hongi.

"Uncle Bob, cool as a cucumber, and mad as a hatter, because they were tampering with the Rolls-Noise." Lan moved his arm gingerly. "And when Mr. Bulke told him about me and the watch, his voice became like broken-off icicles, falling into a tin. Sort of cold, clipped and cutting. 'And why,' he asked, 'have you not informed the police if that is what you suspect?'

"They hummed and hawed a bit at that, and Mr. Bulke said that he didn't want to get the boy into serious trouble. Uncle laughed shortly, and got me to assure them that I hadn't taken the watch. Then we went across to the car, and he gave them a ride into town.

"Mr. Puddick said, 'I don't think he took the watch, sir. He and his friend saved me from drowning the other day. This boy was in the cabin all right, sir, but I don't think a boy like him would steal. That I don't.'

"When they'd gone I told Uncle about the watch. I didn't want them to know that I'd seen it."

"Where's the Rolls-Noise now?" Hongi asked, twisting the Pania statuette in his hands.

"She's round the back, getting a long, cooling drink in her radiator. And talking of cooling drinks, Aunt Jenny left a jug of real grape fruit juice in the refrigerator for us. You thirsty?"

Hongi did not answer. He moved at about the speed of light to the refrigerator. He poured out drinks for both of them.

"Senior Detective Lan?"

"Yes, Senior Detective Hongi?"

Hongi held out the Pania statuette, and pointed mutely to the congealing blood on the back of his hand.

"Your mother's statuette wasn't rough like that. I rubbed my finger along it before you parcelled it up. And, a strange thing, Senior Detective Lan, this one is lighter, and it opens up, and has these unusual scratches on the inside."

"Great jumping grasshoppers! Those are the same—"

"Want a turn on your cart! Mean old thing! You never let me have a turn," screamed Sis's voice from over the fence.

"I do, too," Bruffie protested. "It's you who are mean —"

"There they go," Hongi grinned. "I'll just see their aunt for a moment while they are busy fighting." He put the Pania statuette carefully in his pocket.

In less than five minutes he was back again. "Yes, we may borrow it. Gosh, they're still battling along. I've never know anyone to fight like that, so often." Hongi looked up as Uncle Bob and Aunt Jenny joined them.

"S-sh!" whispered Uncle Bob. "Just listen."

"Meanie!" screamed Sis again.

"This is Jolly Uncle Jack, the children's friend," a new voice came in cheerful, almost oily tones. "This is your jolly uncle, children, come to sunny Napier to take tape recordings for broadcasting in the new children's session. I want to hear you all, but the first ones on our programme are Sis and Bruffie, enjoying their holiday in the sun. Just listen to them now. Just listen to—"

There was a petrified silence from the garden next door. The twins' aunt could be seen standing in her doorway, listening.

Then pandemonium broke out on the tape recorder. The terrible twins on the tape screamed, shouted, kicked, threatened and bullied. Every fight for several days had been recorded. At the end came the oily tones of Jolly Uncle Jack, "And that, children, is how Sis and Bruffie are spending their holiday with their aunt." The tape recorder stopped.

There was a deep and telling silence.

"Oh," a voice only faintly like Sis's came over the fence. "If Dad heard that, he'd flay us."

"If Mum heard it, she'd send us to different boarding schools. We'd never be allowed to come here again. Gosh, I didn't know we sounded like that. Auntie must think we're awful." The sound of deep, shuddering sobs came over the fence. "We'll tell Auntie how sorry we are," Bruffie howled dismally. "Perhaps if we never fight again as long as we live she'd stop that awful Jolly Uncle Jack putting it across on the radio session—" They sobbed in chorus, and still weeping bitterly moved towards the house.

Aunt Jenny looked at Uncle Bob with her eyes all crinkly at the corners, and held out her hand.

"Congratulations!" she smiled.

The telephone shrilled. Aunt Jenny picked up the receiver. "It's for you, Jolly Uncle Jack," she laughed softly.

"All right." Uncle Bob spoke in oily tones into the telephone. "I won't broadcast anything about you and Sis on the main radio link-up, Bruffie, if you both promise never again to fight or scream for no reason. And if I ever hear of you breaking your promise—" He paused, while he winked at Lan and Hongi. "We'll say no more about it then, young fellow." He hung up the receiver.

"Well," Uncle Bob said with deep satisfaction, "I said I'd fix them. They think that their Auntie dialled the radio station. And if it works a miracle in their behaviour, I don't think that small deception will matter."

"I'm sure their aunt is rejoicing greatly," Aunt Jenny laughed.

"Well," Uncle Bob said modestly, "when she spoke on the 'phone she sounded as if she'd come in for a fortune."

"About Pania," Hongi looked at Lan. Lan looked at his uncle.

"Could you come to a meeting at headquarters, Uncle Bob?"

Aunt Jenny smiled at them. "I have an important engagement in the kitchen, so you can have your meeting here in peace."

Lan smiled his gratitude.

"Before we begin," Hongi raised one dark eyebrow, "can anyone tell me where Flying Officer Wuffit is?"

"He's in his kennel, sleeping the sleep of the good and the just," Lan assured him.

They spoke quickly and earnestly. Presently Uncle Bob lit his pipe, and thinking deeply, drew on it in short, sharp puffs. The smell of tobacco mingled with the perfume from a vase of flowers on the table.

"It's a job for the police, boys," Uncle Bob rose, crossed to the telephone, and dialled a number. He spoke a few words, replaced the receiver, and sat down. "They'll ring back," he said quietly.

The time of waiting seemed endless.

Lan's fingers were twining and intertwining as he thought, but the movement hurt his arm, and he stopped abruptly.

He could smell again the closed-in food-paint smell of the ship, and hear the sudden bursts of Mr. Puddick's loud laughter. And then the incredible blue of the sky over the sea. His skin prickled as he thought of the chase down the hillside, and the sudden twist, plunge and fall on to his arm.

Oh, I wish the police would ring back, he thought.

They waited in silence. The minutes moved with leaden feet.

The telephone shrilled loudly. They all jumped. Hongi, at a nod from Uncle Bob, picked up the receiver.

"The police sergeant, Mr. Sherwood." He handed him the telephone.

CHAPTER TEN

THE FASHIONABLE TOURIST

THOMASINA WAS bored. Her shoulders drooped, her feet, thrust into plastic sandals, kicked at imaginary stones. The holiday crowd, surging down Emerson Street in the centre of the city, saw the flame-haired girl gloomily staring at the footpath. They pushed, laughed, and sauntered in the hot afternoon, the women with wide skirts swinging, the men in shorts and sandals.

The hum of chattering holiday-makers enjoying lazy summer days sang as insistent a song as the distant cicada.

Thomasina did not see them. She did not feel the heat of the afternoon sun. She did feel burning rage and frustration because Hongi and Lan had slipped away that morning when she was not looking. They had set out for Clifton and the gannet sanctuary at Cape Kidnappers. Because of the incoming tide it was too late to follow when she discovered their absence.

In her imagination she was now striding along the sand under the tall cliffs, keeping up with Hongi and Lan until at last they reached the nesting-place of thousands upon thousands of gannets. Thomasina aimed another kick at the kerb, and then hopped miserably on one foot, clutching at the other.

"What's the matter, Thomasina?" Aunt Jenny paused. "You look as if the Pied Piper had run off with all the other children."

"It's not as bad as that, Mrs. Sherwood," Thomasina smiled wanly. "You couldn't call Hongi and Lan *all* the children. Going off to Cape Kidnappers without asking me to go! I'd like an adventure, too. I'm just itching for an adventure," she confided.

"Well, let me see," Aunt Jenny looked dreamy. "When I was young I used to love dressing up. Perhaps—"

"Dressing up," Thomasina said slowly, with a smile widening round her mouth. "My aunt has the most fantastic things. She said I could borrow anything I liked as long as I was careful with them. Whoops, Mrs. Sherwood! That was a swell idea. I'll just be getting along. 'Bye, Mrs. Sherwood!"

Aunt Jenny stood for a moment smiling as she listened to the pad, pad of Thomasina's plastic sandals, and watched her snake her way through the crowds.

It might have been about an hour later, in the hottest part of the afternoon, when a slim, languid figure, very fashionably dressed, teetered on too-high heels along Marine Parade. Her face was a mask of studied boredom. Seldom did a glimmer of interest light those carefully shadowed eyes.

I wonder what I look like from the back, thought Thomasina.

Sometimes her skirt, which slowed down her walking speed to the velocity of a galloping snail, seemed to cause her undue annoyance, but otherwise the slim figure remained cold, unmoved.

Over her shoulder was slung a camera, which together with her ultra-fashionable appearance, seemed to hint that she was perhaps a tourist from one of the luxury liners now berthed at Auckland. Perhaps an American?

Many eyes followed her as she inched along the Parade.

She paused at the paddling pools, and watched the children pretending to swim by walking on their hands and crawling in the water. A smile parted her carefully made-up lips.

"Watch out! I'm going to splash you!" a child shouted. The elegant young lady, smiling so pleasantly, stepped back too far, too hastily, tripped on her too-high heels, and sat down suddenly on the wet concrete.

"Oh, golly wallopers, what will Auntie say?" The fashionable little figure struggled to her feet, and turned in a futile attempt to see a large, damp patch, which adorned the back of her skirt. With nervous haste a slim hand, fingernails carefully lacquered, pushed her modish wig into position, but not before a strand of flaming red hair had wormed into sight.

She smiled her thanks to a dozen eager helpers, and stood in the sun for a few moments, drying that tell-tale damp patch.

With studied calm Thomasina continued her promenade.

A car door slammed, and she looked up, startled.

The bald-headed captain and the thin man were hurrying in front of her, striding along Marine Parade towards the stalls and the games.

Ah, Thomasina thought, here's my chance to find out what they're up to. She teetered after them. In her haste she did not notice that another car had stopped—a well-polished, mature, black English car. Nor did she notice the corpulent figure that left the car, a dignified person above surprisingly spindly legs encased in black gaiters.

The fashionable "tourist" and the corpulent ecclesiastic came into sudden and violent collision.

"Oh, my lord!" Thomasina wondered if that were the correct way to address a bishop, after you had collided with him.

The bishop gazed disapprovingly at the dangling earrings, the black wig, the heavy make-up of the somewhat earthly vision before him.

"Don't you remember me, sir? You met me at the school prize-giving. I'm Thomasina—you know, the one with the red hair and the fleas."

"I remember Thomasina perfectly, but surely—?"

"Oh, I don't look like this all the time," Thomasina assured him earnestly, "but Hongi and Lan—Hongi is my cousin—went to see the gannets at Cape Kidnappers, and I didn't know what to do. Then Lan's Aunt Jenny suggested dressing up, and—here I am."

"So I see," the bishop's eyes twinkled as Thomasina adjusted her wig, and tucked in some stray ends of flaming hair.

"I'm sorry I cannoned into you," Thomasina apologised. "Cannoned into a bishop! That's a pun."

The bishop shook with mirth. "And a very good pun, too," he allowed, falling into slow step beside her. "I also have had an adventurous afternoon. I was successful in passing the test for a driving licence a week ago, and have driven here this afternoon. I feel quite elated."

"I'm sure you do," Thomasina agreed warmly. "It must be wonderful to be able to drive. I suppose you can go really fast now."

"Certainly not!" The bishop looked stern. "I seldom exceed fifteen miles an hour."

"Oh!" Then Thomasina brightened. "Lan's uncle has a car that will go sixteen miles an hour—unless it breaks down. You could have races."

"Certainly not!" the bishop said for the second time.

But Thomasina was not listening. She had with lightning speed aimed her camera, and had clicked the shutter on two men hurrying from a parked car. The bald-headed captain and a strange man. They were going back to the Mardi Gras.

"I like taking photos," Thomasina said.

"So do I," the bishop smiled.

"You should see the ones I've taken in Wellington, at Island Bay. Super ones of the rock pools."

"Really? I must take some there, myself. I'll be visiting Wellington in a few days' time," the bishop added.

With the bishop at her side Thomasina turned towards the stalls at the Mardi Gras. The music blared, and the little round pebbles turned beneath her too-high heels. A smell of fried onions stole from one of the caravans. A child stood and stared at the unusual figures before him. His mother, turning to hurry him up, stood and stared, too.

"I often wonder what attracts people to these places," the bishop said mildly.

"I used to like the merry-go-rounds," Thomasina said, wistfully, "when I was young, I mean. But now," she gazed at her pencil slim skirt, "I doubt if I could lever myself up." She grinned, ruefully.

"Here's a stall selling little statuettes of Pania," the bishop paused. "I could send one to my sister. She collects bric-à-brac of that nature."

Thomasina nodded absently. She was busy taking shot after shot of the Pania stall—and of the stallkeeper and of the customers.

Suddenly she froze. At the back of the stall stood the two men, talking earnestly together.

Thomasina glanced warily at the bishop, who was gazing mildly at the merry-go-round. She tip-toed eagerly round to the back of the Pania stall, and stood close to its canvas wall.

As the music throbbed from the merry-go-round in a new tune, Thomasina heard a high, thin voice.

"Those boys, the Maori one and the English one, with his arm in a sling, they went to Cape Kidnappers to-day. I had them shadowed. They'll be coming back to have a look at this stall. Heard them say so myself. Strikes me they know more than is good for them."

"Te Mata Peak is just the place to lose them if they know too much. Nice little drop over that precipice."

"Certainly they know too much."

Thomasina scarcely breathed. She tip-toed back to the bishop, and her fingers with the silver-varnished nails closed tightly on his black sleeve. Surprised, he looked into Thomasina's horror-stricken eyes.

Swiftly she edged him away. Then, looking over her shoulder furtively: "They mean to get Hongi and Lan. They're going to put them over the side of Te Mata Peak. We must do something! Oh, think of something, quick!"

"My child, what do you mean? Who's going to get Hongi and Lan? Surely you are mistaken, Thomasina?"

"No! No, I heard them clearly! Hongi and Lan seem to know some secret. And those men, the bald captain and the thin man are afraid that they'll tell. What'll we do? Oh, what'll we do?"

"There is always the police," the bishop said, gently.

"But we can't get the police to arrest men until they've done something. And if I tell what I overheard, the men will deny it, and get Hongi and Lan some other way. Oh, what'll we do? What'll we do?" Thomasina angrily brushed tears out of her eyes.

"We can wait by the stall until your cousin and his friend appear, and then quietly offer them a ride home," the bishop suggested. "I doubt if anyone would try to kidnap them while they were talking to such—er— worthy looking people as a bishop, and an attractive young lady in a black wig." The bishop's eyes twinkled kindly.

"You don't understand," Thomasina almost stammered in her anxiety. "Those men are dangerous. Somehow Hongi and Lan found out something—something those men are trying to keep secret. And—and—But you don't believe me! You think that someone who is silly enough to enjoy dressing up like this must be silly all through. But I'm not, I tell you! I'm not!"

"I'm sure you're not," the bishop said, soothingly. "When do you expect the boys to come back from seeing the gannets?"

Thomasina consulted her aunt's watch.

"Any time now. Let's wait within sight of the stall, and then we can see what goes on, and save Hongi and Lan."

"We must not arouse suspicion," said the bishop, folding his hands quietly over his stomach. "We must give our earnest attention to the merry-go-round and the stalls. I will not, however, show any interest in the games of —er—skill."

"All right," Thomasina agreed. "And you can't miss Lan and Hongi. Lan speaks with a sort of cut-off English accent, and Hongi is a Maori, and he's very nice underneath when he's not trying to dodge me."

"I see," the bishop said, gazing at the dwindling crowd.

"I wish I hadn't these silly earrings on. And these stupid heels. And all this make-up. And the varnished nails—and—and—everything," Thomasina gulped. "I wish I just had on old shorts and a T-shirt, and sandals. I feel I could do things then," she added, wistfully.

"There is a lot to be said for shorts and sandals, especially in this heat," the bishop gazed wistfully at his gaiters.

They waited in silence. The seconds seemed hours, and the minutes years.

"There's hardly anyone here, now. We've been waiting for *ages*. For—" Thomasina consulted her aunt's watch, "for half an hour."

"They mightn't come here, after all," the bishop unclasped his hands. "Perhaps they've gone home."

"They may have," said Thomasina looking round anxiously. "No sign of them here."

"In that case, Thomasina, I'll drive you home. If you'd prefer we can visit the boys' people, and see if they have returned safely."

"That's a good idea," Thomasina agreed, and followed him, as quickly as her skirt would allow, to the deserted street.

"Everyone seems to have gone home to tea," the bishop

observed as he ushered Thomasina into his shiny, black Austin.

"Is that a map?" Thomasina's eyes travelled to the glove box.

"Yes, that shows Hawkes Bay. I don't know the smaller places very well."

Thomasina was unfolding it with eager, trembling fingers.

"Look, here's Napier." Her eyes searched the maze of lines. "And here's Te Mata Peak. It's—oh!"

The bishop followed Thomasina's petrified stare.

His own eyes widened in horror.

Up till now he had been doubtful of Thomasina's story. Not that he thought she would deliberately lie to him, but perhaps she had a vivid imagination.

Now with his own eyes he saw two boys, one Maori, the other fairer and more slightly built, walking between two men, who were crowding them into a blue car. The taller man had one hand in his pocket, and was pushing something in that pocket into the Maori boy's back.

"It's a gun," the bishop whispered.

"What'll we do? What'll we do?" gasped Thomasina. "If we rush out and try to attack them they might shoot Hongi."

"I couldn't tackle two men, especially when one has a gun. I am not particularly brave, I suppose, but I feel there must be some other way. Perhaps we will be guided to know what to do," the bishop sounded hopeful.

"Oh, Hongi! Oh, Lan!" sobbed Thomasina, in blackest despair.

CHAPTER ELEVEN

TE MATA PEAK

THE BLUE CAR angled out from its parking place, and streaked off through the quiet evening.

"We can't hope to catch up with them," said the bishop as he turned on the ignition, "but at least we know where they're going. It's just possible that they might go the long way through Taradale and Hastings to throw pursuers off the scent."

"I'm sure they never thought of pursuers. There wasn't a soul anywhere. They didn't even see us, as we were in the car."

The bishop cautiously edged his car out from the kerb.

"There isn't a policeman in sight. I have a great respect for the police," he sighed, "but if we go hunting up the police we might lose track of the boys completely, or be too late."

"Faster! Faster!" Thomasina sobbed, watching the speedometer crawl from five miles to fifteen miles an hour. The bishop responded by increasing his speed to twenty miles an hour.

"We'll go by Te Awa and Clive and through Havelock North to Te Mata Peak," he said, gently.

"Those awful men will probably go that way, too." Thomasina sat on the extreme edge of the seat, peering in front of her, hoping against hope that she would have another glimpse of the blue car.

"Faster! Faster!" she urged again, rubbing away the rain of tears, and smearing her thickly applied eye shadow.

The bishop gripped the steering wheel tightly, and tensed every muscle. Then, having shut his eyes for the split fraction of a second, he put his foot firmly on the accelerator, and kept it there.

The car rocketted forward like some atomic missile.

"Wonderful!" breathed Thomasina, holding on hard. She did not see the railway line on one side of the road, nor the sea. She saw the ribbon of road before them, and rushing away beneath them. Mile after mile. Her tears dried on her cheeks, and her lips parted in breathless anxiety.

"We might get there in time." The bishop's breath was coming in short, sharp gasps, as if he had been running in some life and death race. His foot remained firm on the accelerator, and the answering Austin lunged through the quiet evening.

Before they reached Clive, the road curved, and snaked inland towards Havelock North.

They were oblivious of the beautiful houses and gardens, the brick terraces, the stone walls, the purple and magenta and yellow flowers, the willows and poplars and blue-gum trees, and the smooth, rolling green lawns.

Neither the bishop nor Thomasina spoke. The car began to climb. Up and up. And farther up the winding road. Sometimes the side fell away steeply—down, down to a fertile valley far below. The road narrowed now as it spiralled around the mountain. Its rough surface jolted the straining Austin, slowing it down on its upward path. The wind blew in wild gusts.

"I feel—I feel, round every corner there's something waiting to pounce," Thomasina gasped.

As they reached the end of the road to Te Mata Peak, the bishop's neatly shod foot on the accelerator faltered for the first time. There, quietly parked on the grassy hillside, stood the blue car.

Startled, the two men in the front seat stared at the black Austin. In a split second Thomasina's camera clicked twice, recording the scene.

Then, after muttering vehemently to the boys, white-faced and tight-lipped in the back of the car, the men got out and strolled slowly to the edge of the peak, as if to admire the scenery.

The wind, completely calm in Havelock North, rushed with renewed force across the hillside. The captain clamped his cap to his head with an impatient hand. The thin man, hatless, stood for a second, as the gale struck him, wildly swirling his lank hair.

"What'll we do? What'll we do?" Thomasina whispered loudly against the moaning wind.

The bishop did not answer immediately. "I don't know," he said sadly, at length. "If we take the boys, there's no knowing what they'd do with that gun. If we confront the men and demand they free them, they'd probably laugh at us. There isn't another soul in sight, either."

Thomasina's breath came in little gulping sobs.

The men, with many a backward glance at the boys, sitting petrified in the blue car, struggled slowly against the wind towards the fence at the edge of the precipice.

"I —I don't think I can bear this," Thomasina sobbed wildly. Her hand smeared the eye shadow on to her face, and mingled it with her tears. "To find them, and then not to be able to do anything. We've—I've—perhaps if we—"

"Perhaps I could edge the car so they couldn't see the boys—"

"And I could open our car door and try to get them inside, quickly—" Thomasina looked furtively at the blue car.

"I'd have to distract the men's attention." The bishop moved restlessly.

"But—but they have a gun!"

"We've got to do our best for Hongi and Lan."

"I'll distract their attention," Thomasina offered. "I've done it before. I'll—"

"You'll do nothing of the sort," the bishop said with unwonted severity. "Just get the boys into our car, and perhaps, if right prevails—"

"Yes," Thomasina breathed fervently, "Yes, oh, yes."

The bishop turned his car gently, until it stood alongside the blue car, obscuring it from the men's eyes.

Thomasina nodded to the bishop's inquiring glance, and sat motionless while, with quiet dignity, he left the car, and strolled towards the two men.

He knows they have a gun, Thomasina thought, watching the almost grotesquely rotund figure in black climbing on its thin legs over the wind-flattened grass. I think he must be the very bravest man I've ever met.

Silently she inched open the back door nearest the boys, and turning towards them, slowly and deliberately winked.

They gaped at the smudged, tear-stained face of the

girl in the Austin. No flicker of recognition passed over their faces. Lan stared, feeling vaguely that he had seen someone wink like that before.

"Such an interesting view," the bishop greeted the men chattily. He stared down at the rock face falling sheer below them. "Quite like German castles and Egyptian pyramids. Wonderful view."

"Wonderful," the thin man growled, making an effort.

"Wonderful," echoed the captain, a forced smile breaking the putty-like smoothness of his face, and one foot tapping impatiently. All this time he had kept his right hand seemingly clenched over something in his coat pocket.

"And there's the Tuki Tuki River," the bishop beamed on them both. He stood gazing his fill of the view.

"You can see Havelock North," the thin man seemed pleasantly determined to allay suspicion.

"And Napier and the breakwater and the sea," the captain added, not to be outdone.

"And the snow-streaked peaks of Ruapehu, I'm sure," the bishop leaned against the fence at the edge of the precipice. "A wonderful view."

"Too right," the thin man said, with affected enthusiasm.

The wind sat, as it were, on its haunches, waiting. The captain unclamped his hand from his cap, and half turned, as if to go back to the car. A sudden gust seemed to seize its advantage, and shrieking, lifted his cap from his head, and flung it over the fence. It perched on a jutting rock about a yard below the fence, just out of reach.

"Would you like to get it?" he suggested to the thin man.

"Me get it? What would I want to do a fool thing like that for? Me get it?" he repeated. "Don't be silly. I might get blown over."

Another violent sweep of the roaring wind confirmed his words.

Muttering angrily beneath his breath the captain at last took his right hand out of his pocket, and swung one leg over the fence. He bent down for his cap. The wind playfully moved it just out of reach.

"Come on," said the thin man, rivetting his eyes on the captain inching down the precipice.

The bishop's head turned for a split second in the direction of the two cars. Then he gave his undivided attention to the captain.

"How plucky you must be," he said, kindly. "It is not everyone who would dare a precipice like this one."

The captain muttered words that were blown away by the rushing wind.

The thin man leaned over the fence.

"Hold on to that rock, and you'll reach it, yet," he instructed. "Nasty drop, that," he said, chattily.

The captain edged an inch nearer his cap. His fingers clutched, and grasped the encircling braid.

"Got it!" he gloated, crawling upwards. The wind flattened the grasses beside him. Like an actor in a slow motion film he carefully climbed over the fence at the top of the cliff.

"And now," the bishop hastily felt in his waistcoat pocket, "I wonder if you would be interested in cigars, my friends?" He triumphantly produced two cigars from the inner recesses of his coat. "So many people press cigars on me at official dinners. These are of particularly fine quality, I believe."

The men took the gift with alacrity.

In the bishop's car Thomasina beckoned with one scarcely moving finger, and slowly, slowly the back door of the blue car edged open. Thomasina studied the scenery with absorbed interest. The howling wind broke the stillness.

The weight of two additional bodies lurched the Austin almost imperceptibly. Without turning Thomasina smoothly shut the door. Then leaning out, as if to study the mud-guards, Thomasina pressed the back door of the blue car gently shut.

"It is time I went my way," the bishop said, quaintly, and smiled at one and then the other. "I will leave you to contemplate this magnificent scenery."

"Thanks a lot," the thin man smiled, showing yellowed teeth.

"Thanks again," the captain parted his lips with studied goodwill.

The smoke of the cigars richly scented the air.

The bishop ambled slowly to the Austin. Without glancing in the back of the car, or showing the slightest interest in anything but the ignition, he settled himself in the driving seat.

For a split second he turned and raised questioning eyebrows at Thomasina. She nodded imperceptibly. The bishop started the car and glided slowly over the grass.

The men at the edge of the precipice puffed their cigars, and gave their earnest attention to the scenery.

The bishop drove with the deliberation of a tortoise going to get its breakfast.

"Faster! Faster!" Thomasina begged.

"If I hurried," the bishop smiled slightly, "those men might think I had something to hide."

Nor did a shout from behind them cause him to increase his speed. On the contrary he slowed down with calm circumspection. It was only when he saw in his rear vision mirror that the men were searching the hillside, and that the blue car was not following, that he hurried slightly.

"They seem to be looking for the boys up on the hill-side," he pondered aloud.

He continued to drive with painstaking care. A car horn shrieked behind them, and the bishop cautiously moved to a wider part of the road, and stopped while the blue car screamed past.

"They seem in rather a hurry," he observed mildly.

"Hurray! They've gone!" Thomasina shouted, in her relief.

"We're not safe yet," the bishop reminded her. "At any moment—"

"At any moment we'll be down from this hill, and streaking back home again," Thomasina jigged up and down with delight.

"O-oh, look!" she pointed at the two figures, who were jacking up the back of the now stationary blue car. "They've got a puncture."

"And no spare tyre, from the look of it," the bishop increased his speed slightly.

They were almost past the blue car before they were noticed.

"Send us out a spare tyre from Havelock!" shouted the captain, waving wildly.

The bishop seemed suddenly very hard of hearing.

"SEND US A SPARE TYRE!" bellowed the thin man.

But the bishop had rounded a corner, and with his foot firmly on the accelerator was streaking towards Napier.

"Please may we sit up now?" came a muffled voice from the back.

"Certainly," the bishop increased his speed.

"We have never," Hongi and Lan spoke as with one voice, "been so petrified in our lives. How on earth did you find out what was going on?"

"Your cousin told me, Hongi," the bishop smiled as if at some secret joke.

"You know my name? And my cousin? But I've only the one cousin in Napier. Red-haired Thomasina. Gosh, you could just about light a fire with her hair," Hongi grinned, as if forcing away the terror that still surrounded them. "She couldn't have told you. We gave her the slip this morning when we went to Cape Kidnappers."

"A singularly appropriate name," the bishop smiled.

"We'd have given anything to see Thomasina when those men got us," Lan confessed, nursing his sprained arm as needles of pain shot through it.

"Well, she saw you, and insisted that I do something. And, not content with that, she rescued you herself."

"Oh, I didn't. You rescued them. I've never seen anyone so brave." Thomasina turned her somewhat smeared eyes to him.

"I don't understand it at all, but I've never been so grateful in my life," Lan assured them.

"Nor have I," Hongi swallowed hard. "And what did you say about rescuing us? That Thomasina rescued us? But she's got red hair, and—"

"But her aunt," Thomasina turned dancing eyes on them, "never dyes her hair. She wears wigs. Very fashionable things at present—wigs." And with a slight smile she swept off the black wig. As a cascade of glowing red hair flowed round her face, Hongi gasped:

"Thomasina!"

"Thomasina!" gurgled Lan.

"Jumping Jupiter!" exclaimed Hongi, leaning over the front seat and pumping her hand violently.

"Golly-gosh!" Lan blew his nose loudly, as if he were overcome with some deep emotion.

"It was the bishop," Thomasina assured them, quietly. "He was so noble that he didn't even mind going to see the Mardi Gras with me in this foolish outfit. If he hadn't come nothing would have gone right."

"We think you both were noble," Hongi beamed at her.

Lan, suddenly feeling tired about the mouth, realised that he had been smiling as widely as possible for several minutes.

"I'll take you all home," announced the bishop glancing at the shimmering sea. "Lovely evening, isn't it?"

"Super, eh?" Hongi grinned.

"Duper!" Lan agreed.

"Scrumtedelicious!" Thomasina purred.

They could hear the shrill of the telephone as the black

Austin crunched over the gravel driveway to the open front door.

Then Aunt Jenny's voice, sharp with horror:

"Bob! Thomasina's missing now. First the boys, and now Thomasina! They should have been home hours ago!"

"Don't worry, Jenny, I'll go—Good gracious!" Uncle Bob's voice tailed into silence as he looked through the doorway.

Aunt Jenny stood tranfixed as first Lan, and then Hongi catapulted out of the back of the car. They were followed by a strange figure teetering along on too high heels, in a too narrow skirt, and carrying a black wig. With her, rubbing his hands, and beaming with goodwill, came the rotund bishop.

Aunt Jenny opened her mouth like a goldfish in a bowl, and silently shut it again.

Uncle Bob removed his pipe from his mouth, and silently put it back again.

While Thomasina and Hongi, with shrill, excited voices reassured their relations over the telephone, Lan and the bishop began the story.

"That settles it once and for all," Uncle Bob said when he had heard Thomasina's and Hongi's version also. His mouth was a grim hard line. "I'm going to the police."

CHAPTER TWELVE

THE ROLLS-NOISE SETS FORTH

THE SMELL of coffee, fried eggs and bacon drifted through the dark house.

"Mmm!" Lan sniffed, turning his head. "Breakfast!" He stretched slightly, and stretching, fell more soundly asleep.

"Wake up! Wake up, Lan!" Uncle Bob's hand was shaking his shoulder. "Time to get up!"

"Mmm," Lan muttered in his sleep. "Time to go—" He went on snoring gently, like a kitten on a summer's day.

"Come on, Lan! Breakfast's ready!"

Lan cautiously opened one eye, and shut it again.

"Still dark. Dreaming," he said, loudly and clearly, before he went to sleep again.

"Lan Sherwood, either you wake up, or I tip a bucket of water over you," his uncle's deep voice said with threatening determination. "And if that fails I can always toss you in a bath—full of cold water, of course," he promised grimly.

"Bath?" Lan sat up. "What on earth's the matter, Uncle Bob? It's still the middle of the night."

"Get up, Lan. Breakfast's ready."

"But it's still the middle of the night," Lan said again, looking at the darkness framed in his window.

Uncle Bob crossed to the window, pulled down the blind with an impatient jerk, and switched on the light.

"We don't want anyone to suspect what is going on," he said turning to his nephew.

Lan stared speechlessly. "Why—what?" he stammered, gazing at the tweed suit his uncle wore. Why wasn't he in shorts, as usual? Why breakfast when it was still dark?

Uncle Bob sat on the edge of the bed. His eyes were deep with concern. "I've seen the police, Lan." He raked through his hair with nervous fingers.

"To-night?"

"Last night when you went to bed. This is the very early morning now. They're charging the captain and his friend with possessing an unregistered firearm, but they want to see if they can trick them into giving away the smuggling secret. That is, if they really are involved in it. It looks mighty suspicious, but none of us has any real proof. Just suspicions."

"But what if those men try to kidnap us again?" Lan shivered. The depths from the top of Te Mata Peak seemed darker and more terrible as he remembered them.

"The police want us to spirit you away where you'd be safe for a few days. Right away from Napier until the *Golden Star* sails for England."

Lan sniffed. "Is that why—?"

"Yes, that's why there's bacon and eggs ready now. Get up, Lan. You're going to Wellington, and Hongi, Thomasina, Aunt Jenny and I are going, too. And Wuffit's going, as well."

"All of us? In the Rolls-Noise? There wouldn't be room, would there?"

"No, our new friend, the bishop, has offered to take half the party on the strict condition that he is not expected to drive at more than sixteen miles an hour."

"Gosh! How long will it take?"

"About two hundred and thirteen miles at sixteen miles an hour—" Uncle Bob began to work it out mentally.

"About fourteen hours," Lan announced, triumphantly first with the answer. "That is, barring accidents."

"Just over thirteen hours," his uncle amended. "We're leaving at half-past four. We should be out of Napier before anyone is up, or has time to suspect." Uncle Bob paused. "Hongi's grandfather is on holiday, but he'll lend us his house at Island Bay in Wellington. Hongi's mother won't be able to come. She's working. Thomasina will go home, of course, but she lives at Island Bay, too, so I'm sure you'll be seeing her."

"I'm sure we shall," Lan grinned, jumping out of bed. "I certainly was delighted to see Thomasina, not that I recognised her then, and the bishop on Te Mata Peak. I'd have grovelled with pleasure." He made towards the bathroom. "I won't need that sling. My arm feels fine. Won't be long, Uncle Bob."

Eleven hours and one puncture later, "Another flat tyre," Uncle Bob said in a voice as flat as the tyre. "It's the finish of things until I can get a spare."

"Oh, dear," the bishop peered from the Austin.

A car honked suddenly, and with a scream of brakes a blue car jerked to a halt.

"Well, well," said Mr. Bulke pleasantly, easing out of the driver's seat, "and what have we here? Sherwood's old bomb, I said to myself, and all the family, too."

He was greeted by a dead silence.

"Just as well it broke down on the main road. Cars

passing all the time. Didn't expect to be here myself, but the owner of this car rang me up last night, and insisted, positively insisted that I take it for a little holiday in Wellington."

The silence was becoming embarrassing, but Mr. Bulke did not notice it.

"Anyhow, I can give you a lift into Wellington," Mr. Bulke opened the car door with a flourish.

"Thank you very much," the bishop said with old world courtesy, as he stepped from the Austin, "but my very good friends are honouring me with their company."

Mr. Bulke smiled doubtfully, and shut the car door.

"You're going to Wellington? Perhaps I'll see you there?"

Under cover of stowing the luggage from the Rolls-Noise in the bishop's car Uncle Bob said nothing, but Aunt Jenny smiled largely.

"You can throw sticks for Wuffit," she said kindly, as Uncle Bob bundled her into the car. "And we'll be staying at Island Bay," she raised her voice in case he should not hear her above the noise of the engine, "right on the seafront near the playground." Suddenly she clapped her hand over her mouth, "I'm so tired I don't know what I'm saying."

"Jenny," Uncle Bob said, as the bishop placed his camera in a safer place, and waved him into the driver's seat, "that's torn it." He glared, ferociously. "Torn it right in two."

The Austin, with Uncle Bob at the wheel, eased into gear, and leaped towards Wellington and Island Bay.

CHAPTER THIRTEEN

ISLAND BAY

THE FOLLOWING morning, a southerly wind, blowing straight from the Antarctic, cooled Island Bay. The sea whooshed over the rough brown rocks making white suds of foam, and the fishing boats rocked at anchor in the brilliant blue water.

"What's that little island?" Lan asked, from his perch astride the front fence.

"It's called Tapu-te-Ranga," Hongi said quietly.

"Anyhow, it's a recreation reserve." Thomasina had joined them, and stood sniffing the salty air. "Fish," she smiled a wide cat smile. "You can just about smell it at Island Bay. Lots of fishermen live here, and they're interesting, because so many of them are Italians. Large brown eyes and dark hair, you know. The Italian girls are really pretty."

"It's got a look of the Mediterranean," said Lan and he seemed to drink in the blue of the sky, and the sparkling blue of the sea.

"Makes you sort of lifted up inside." Hongi smelled the cool air, and pushed his shoulders back as he gazed in delight at the surging sea, splintering on the rocks.

"Mighty nice of your grandfather to let us have this place for a few days," Lan said as he cautiously moved his position to another spike on the fence.

"Very kind," Thomasina agreed.

"Children," Aunt Jenny, wearing a blue flowered dress, came on silent feet from the house, "I don't want you to go out of sight, nor to speak to anyone here that you don't know. Uncle Bob and I are taking no chances. This is a wonderful place for a holiday, but this is not a holiday. Not anything like one. Putting it bluntly, we're just plain scared."

"We are, too," Hongi assured her. "I didn't think anyone could be as frightened as we were on Te Mata Peak. We'll take every precaution, though we won't need to," he added, with a grin, "because we're just going to stay put where precautions won't be necessary."

"Good boy," Aunt Jenny approved. "It'll be dull for you, but—" her eyes widened. "It's not Mr. Bulke in that blue car, is it? Quick! Inside, all of you!"

"Hallo, there!" a hearty voice interrupted their head-long flight. "Mrs. Sherwood, isn't it?" The blue car slowed down as Mr. Bulke leaned out and hailed them. "Don't know anyone else in Wellington, so I thought I'd look you up. The directions you gave me were clear enough to lead me to you first go off."

Lan groaned under his breath.

"Lucky you were all out in the garden, or I might have missed you," said Mr. Bulke, beaming with pleasure, as he swung out of the car.

Aunt Jenny's smile was distinctly strained.

"Here, Wuffit, good dog! Fetch it!" In boisterous good humour Mr. Bulke threw a piece of driftwood.

Wuffit, hearing his name, came bounding out from behind the house, tongue lolling, eyes snapping with delight at a game, and crazy excitement in every paw.

"Won't you—won't you sit down, Mr. Bulke?" Aunt

Jenny indicated a canvas garden chair, as if it were a poisonous snake.

"Delighted! De-delighted," he repeated doubtfully as the canvas sagged alarmingly under his weight. "Just the day for a cup of tea."

"Er—yes, of course," Aunt Jenny fled into the house.

Lan, Hongi and Thomasina seemed to have disappeared, but Wuffit, with delighted goodwill, was smelling round Mr. Bulke's trouser turn-ups.

"Here, fetch it, Wuffit! Good boy!" From Mr. Bulke's hand a piece of wood described a wide arc in the air. With eyes glued on the wood Wuffit sped on galloping paws.

"Gosh," exclaimed Hongi, watching from a window. "There goes Wuffit, at the speed of light, straight into the fuchsia bush."

"No one, to see Mr. Bulke throwing sticks for Wuffit, would think he was so awful," Thomasina added, thoughtfully.

"We haven't proof that he was connected with those men who tried to kidnap us. Though he's so friendly with them they let him use their car. We've only suspicions," Lan's eyes were steely grey.

"Yes, he's pally with them all right, and it was no accident that he turned up when we were on our way to Wellington," said Thomasina drumming her fingers on the window ledge.

"It could be explained," Hongi meditated out loud. "Perhaps the owner of the car lent it to Mr. Bulke out of goodness of heart."

"You make me laugh," Lan assured him, coldly.

"And we were on the main highway," Hongi ignored

Lan's incredulity. "Lots of cars must have seen us, I suppose."

"And what about all this friendliness, this coming out to see us?" Thomasina raised her eyebrows as she glared at Hongi.

"It could be that he was lonely. Lots of people on ships must be lonely in ports where they know no one," Hongi persisted. "Mind you, I don't believe things are all right, but I'm trying to look at it from all sides."

"Hongi's right," Lan grinned ruefully. "I'm so one-eyed about them that I can't see any possible good people at all in that outfit. I don't mind admitting I was never so frightened in my life as I was on Te Mata Peak. I guess it's sort of warped my views a bit."

"Too right," Hongi agreed. "There's another thing we have to see about—Thomasina."

"I'm not a thing," Thomasina protested.

"Yes, that's right," Lan grinned at her. "I was talking to Uncle last night about admitting her to our Junior C.I.B."

"So that's what it is?" Thomasina's eyes gleamed.

"And he's willing? We can tell her all about—?"

"Yes, if we want Thomasina as a full member he's willing she should know all about the smuggling, after rescuing us like that. He thinks she's proved herself a very worthy member of such a brilliant organisation. Those were his very words," Lan said, modestly.

"I agree," Hongi patted Thomasina vigorously on the back.

"I agree, too." Lan pumped Thomasina's hand.

"Cheers! Now I can stop stalking you," Thomasina smiled warmly. "I've got some evidence, too. I got some super shots with my camera of those men on Te Mata. The blue car and the two of you were with the men, of course."

A piece of wood struck the window lightly. A scrabble of paws followed over the pathway to find it.

They watched Wuffit's wild hunting for his target in the flower bed.

"Ah, Uncle Bob's entertaining Mr. Bulke," Lan announced with relief. "I was wondering how long we could ignore him, even if we do suspect him very gravely."

"I'm just dying to hear about the smuggling, but we'd better go and help Aunt Jenny. We don't want it said that we bravely left others to confront the suspect while we retired to hide in the lounge," Thomasina grimaced.

"We'd certainly better go," Hongi and Lan agreed together.

"It'd be wiser not to let him know we suspect him," Lan added, thoughtfully.

"Just you watch me," Thomasina winked one large and twinkling eye.

"She's up to something," Hongi groaned. "I never trust that wink."

Thomasina hurried to the kitchen, and in a few minutes swept out with a tray of morning tea cups, the teapot and a jug of milk.

"And may I trouble you for the sugar?" she called to Lan, now hesitating in the doorway, in effusively dulcet tones. Thomasina poured Mr. Bulke's tea, not too strong, the exact distance from the top of the cup, and with the grace and ease of one who, since infancy, was accustomed to dispensing tea in the best circles.

"Galloping catfish! Just look at Thomasina," Hongi

said in an aside to Aunt Jenny, as she came out of the house. "Acting as if she's Lady Pushen-Hyphen-Sneezit at the mayoral garden party."

Aunt Jenny hid a smile, and hurried to join the people on the lawn.

Uncle Bob stood up, and went to get another chair, while Mr. Bulke gallantly eased, with a creaking, swaying movement, out of the deck chair.

"Nice little place you've got here," he observed as he again settled his rather shiny, navy-blue suit in the creaking deck chair. "Staying long?"

"Er—we're not sure yet," Aunt Jenny stammered, and nervously began to pour him another cup of tea, until she realised his cup was almost full.

"What's happened to that old bomb of a car of yours?" Mr. Bulke turned his plump, ruddy face to Uncle Bob as he came back with another deck chair.

"Oh, that's stranded at Levin." Uncle Bob paused. "I don't intend to drive her back to Napier. I've rung a garage to fix up her tyres, and to rail her to Napier. I'll have to return her to her real owner soon. Not that he ever uses her. Just keeps her on his father's farm like a family pet."

"How are you all getting back, then? Could I give you a lift in that car I've borrowed?"

"Oh, very good of you, but we've planned to return by air," Uncle Bob said, hastily.

"By air?" Hongi gasped, spilling the sugar. "I've never been in an aeroplane. But what about the bishop?"

"He'll stay in Wellington for a time to recover from his recent surfeit of driving," a smile passed swiftly over Uncle Bob's suntanned face. "Then he may return north or go on to Christchurch, or the West Coast. He hasn't decided yet."

Aunt Jenny poured more tea.

Soon Mr. Bulke rose reluctantly, threw a last stick for Wuffit, thanked them for their kindness, and said, smiling broadly, "Well, I'll be seeing you again."

The blue car bore him away.

"I suppose he's already told those men in Napier, the captain and the thin man, where we are," Thomasina said and impatiently tossed her glowing hair out of her eyes.

The telephone in the house rang shrilly.

"I'll take it," Lan raced Thomasina to the door.

"It's the bishop," he mouthed silently to Thomasina. "Yes, sir, we'll certainly do that. Yes, we did find it exciting. Yes, here's Uncle now." He handed the receiver to Uncle Bob.

"The bishop wants us to write him the story of our adventures. I promised we would," he told Hongi and Thomasina, when they were washing and drying the dishes.

"Too right," Hongi grinned, and jerked his head sideways in agreement. "I'd do anything he wanted us to."

"You couldn't meet a nicer bishop," Thomasina said, with dancing eyes, in her best party voice.

Uncle Bob paused in the kitchen doorway.

"Anything wrong?" asked Aunt Jenny looking up anxiously.

Thomasina paused with the dish-mop in her hand.

Hongi held the plate he was wiping.

Lan left the cupboard door half open as he waited.

"A shipping strike. It was reported in the paper. The

bishop drew my attention to it. The *Golden Star* won't be sailing until the strike is settled."

"O-oh! What'll you do, then?" Thomasina paused as she washed the last plate.

Uncle Bob stared unseeingly at the wet dishes on the bench.

"It's a problem, all right. If they're in Napier I certainly don't want to take you children back there. On the other hand, they must know where you are now. I can't see Bulke keeping that information to himself."

"You've got to go back to work soon, too," Aunt Jenny added.

"We've certainly got something to think about," Uncle Bob chewed on the end of his pipe. "In the meantime, till we decide, what about a picnic on that islet in the bay?" He jerked his head towards the window, and five heads craned to see.

"It looks wonderful," Aunt Jenny studied it joyfully. "All grassy, and rocky like a tiny mountain with the waves breaking over its brown rock feet."

"How shall we get there?" Lan wiped the last plate.

"I've managed to hire a small boat with an outboard motor," Uncle Bob said.

"I love boats and waves all blue with white foam like soap on them," Thomasina smiled widely.

"Well, we'll forget Mr. Bulke and our suspicions and we'll have a picnic on the island." Uncle Bob turned to Thomasina and asked, "Do you know what it's called?"

"Yes, Hongi and I spent a long time one holiday asking people and reading up books about it."

"It's called Tapu-te-Ranga," said Hongi as he moved to the table to help butter bread for sandwiches.

"Hongi wasn't sure of the meaning, so we asked a Maori friend about it, and we learnt that it probably meant 'sacred fishing-ground'." Thomasina chopped up lettuce as she spoke. "'Tapu' means sacred."

"But the most exciting part was when we found an old book by Elsdon Best, called 'Land of Tara'. And what do you know! It had lots about that little island. Come to think of it, I suppose Island Bay was called after that island."

"What did the book say?" Aunt Jenny paused with the butter knife in mid-air.

"Well, the local Maoris used to go there for refuge when they were attacked by a raiding party. Of course it's a very old name in Maori stories. There was a very famous tapu house, Wharekura, in the old homeland of the Maori, and that was the name of its site."

"In the Napier Inner Harbour, Watchman Isle has the same native name, so this little island may have been called after that," Uncle Bob said.

"I like the story best about Tamatea-ariki-nui, the Polynesian voyager," Thomasina said. "He came in his canoe about five or six hundred years ago, and he carried three lizards in a calabash. One lizard escaped at Ahuriri, Napier. And that adventurous lizard was called Tapu-te-Ranga. I'm sure the island was named after him."

"Why, we've finished getting the lunch ready," Aunt Jenny smiled. "Now for Tapu-te-Ranga Island. It's not far."

When they were seated in the boat, Uncle Bob jerked the lanyard, again and yet again. The engine spluttered, choked and then throbbed evenly.

"Look at the waves!" Thomasina stared at the ever

widening wash from the boat. Wuffit thumped his tail wildly.

The houses on the shore began to look smaller, while the island looked larger.

"I'd like to go for a run a bit farther out if the weather holds," said Uncle Bob crinkling his eyes against the sun. "Weather forecast wasn't too good this morning."

"There are a few clouds, and the wind is cold," Aunt Jenny said shivering slightly in the sunshine.

The boat phut-phutted towards the island.

"Don't move, Aunt Jenny," Lan warned, as she tried to get up. "You should sit still in boats."

"Of course. But why does that man jump and shout?"

"Man jump and shout?" Thomasina glanced towards Aunt Jenny, and then followed where her eyes were watching. "My goodness, Hongi, it's Mr. Bulke on the beach, and he's acting as if we were the Christmas turkeys that ran away. My word, is he excited!"

With one accord they turned and gazed at Mr. Bulke shouting and gesticulating on the shore.

Wuffit barked a sharp reply.

"Perhaps," Lan suggested, "he was intending to kidnap us."

"Perhaps," Uncle Bob meditated aloud, "it would be a good idea to have our cruise around now, to give him time to go away. Then we can enjoy our picnic on the island in comparative peace."

"Good idea," Aunt Jenny said, shrugging into her coat, "It's quite cold, though. Is that a sort of greyness over the sun?"

"There's something coming all right." Uncle Bob's forehead creased as he watched the deepening shadow of clouds dull the blue brilliance of the day. "Probably the rain will be on us before we know it."

"Wouldn't we have time for a look-see first?" Hongi's eyes were pleading.

"I'm sure we could. We'll keep an eye on the weather. We're not far out, anyway," Aunt Jenny said.

Lan peered over the side of the boat. The sea had changed colour and had a battleship grey tinge in the blueness. The waves were small, and sometimes with little white crests. The water smelled colder and saltier.

Or can't you smell cold things? Lan thought. Only I'm sure I can.

The boat bucketted suddenly. Aunt Jenny gave a small scream of alarm, and clung to the seat. Wuffit howled dismally.

"It's getting choppy, isn't it?" Uncle Bob gazed back at Tapu-te-Ranga.

The wind gave a low howl, and the boat began to pitch as it faced the incoming sea. A wave broke over the bow.

"I'm soaking wet," Thomasina tried to brush the water off her dress. "Ow, it's gone right through, and it's co-old." She shivered, and huddled nearer to Aunt Jenny.

"It looks as if it's really going to be a storm," Uncle Bob's eyes looked dark and foreboding under their bushy eyebrows. "So it's home again, and we'll leave Tapu-te-Ranga for another day."

Another wave, higher than the last, confirmed his decision. For a moment it seemed as if a grey wall of water was engulfing them. Wuffit cowered near Lan.

"Home it certainly is," Uncle Bob said tersely.

"And quickly," Aunt Jenny added, holding on tightly to the seat.

"Phut-phut," the engine said, and suddenly was silent.

"Oars!" Uncle Bob fiddled with the engine in a vain attempt to make it re-start.

"There aren't any. Should there be?" Sea-spray ran down Aunt Jenny's face.

"Oars? Of course there should. That fool of a man must have forgotten them. I should have seen to it myself before I hired the boat."

"Perhaps," Lan said with chattering teeth, "they were taken away."

"Perhaps Mr. Bulke—" Thomasina voiced the suspicion that had taken possession of them.

"He's a seaman. He'd have known about the storm. Seamen get to know about the weather." Hongi clenched his fists as he gazed over the whitecapped, swelling waves. "There's no one about now. They've all gone in out of the storm. Even if we shouted it'd do no good."

"There's a launch going in. Shout now!" Aunt Jenny's voice sounded eerie above the noise of the wind.

Their voices in unison flew over the restless sea.

"Look! They've seen us! They're waving and laughing." Aunt Jenny laughed in her relief.

"They aren't coming! They think we're only fooling. Dare-devils enjoying the excitement of the storm." Uncle Bob's clenched fist came down on his other hand.

Another wave crashed, and the boat lurched lopsidedly.

"I—I think I'm going to be sick," Thomasina said, huskily. "Yes, I—"

Aunt Jenny held her while the boat heaved, and Lan and Hongi tried to bale out the seawater with their sunhats, and a tin labelled "Whole Tomatoes", that lay in the stern.

No one spoke. Uncle Bob jerked the lanyard to re-start the engine. He tried over and over again. Once, as if in mockery, the engine gave a faint cough, then was still.

Lan and Hongi, with clenched teeth, baled furiously with the tin and the hats.

Aunt Jenny's lips moved silently.

The boat hesitated, and pitched forward dizzily on the wave crest.

No one spoke.

"If only we could reach Tapu-te-Ranga," Uncle Bob passed a weary hand over his forehead.

No one answered.

Through the noise of the waves and the wind came a faint new sound. The steady phut-phut, phut-phut of a launch engine.

"They won't see us." Thomasina's face looked old and gaunt as she spoke.

"Ready, now! Shout!" Uncle Bob ordered.

Their loudest shouts seemed thin and puny as they mingled with the screaming wind.

They shouted again and again, and waved wildly.

A thin, answering cry was borne on the wind.

"Ahoy, there! AHOY!"

"AHOY! AHOY! AHOY!"

The boat came nearer, and an arm waved.

At the same moment they recognised the man in the shiny, navy-blue suit.

"Mr. Bulke!" breathed Thomasina. "We're caught. He can do anything he likes to get rid of us." She turned aside and crouched lower in the boat.

The knotted end of a rope struck the gunwale, and Hongi grasped at it wildly, and secured it firmly.

"Ready?" Mr. Bulke shouted, his voice fading to a thin wall. "TOW YOU IN," he roared, in a sudden lull in the shrieking wind.

The rope jerked tight, the boat slowly followed the pulling line. The waves lifted and dropped them in valleys of water like the hills and hollows of a scenic railway.

Thomasina breathed in little soft gasps. Lan's straining eyes narrowed as he watched the tugging rope. With the empty tin Hongi started to bale again. Wuffit raised his head, but crouched down, miserably.

Aunt Jenny's lips still moved in silence, but the words she framed were of deep thankfulness. Only Uncle Bob looked puzzled and undecided.

The jagged rocks of Tapu-te-Ranga loomed wet with the dashing spray and the mounting waves.

In front of them Mr. Bulke steered his launch through the western channel between the island and the shore, and towed them into the calmer waters of the Bay.

CHAPTER FOURTEEN

ROCK POOLS

THE WARMTH inside the house came to meet them as they opened the door.

"Get your wet things off, and I'll hurry with the tea," said Aunt Jenny going towards the kitchen.

"We'll all help." Uncle Bob followed, and washed his hands at the kitchen sink, and, rinsing off the yellow soap, dried them vigorously on the red striped towel.

Mr. Bulke lowered himself heavily into a rung-backed kitchen chair. "What I couldn't make out," he said slowly, with narrowed eyes, "was why you took no notice at first when I hailed you before the storm."

There was a deep silence.

What'll we say? Lan thought, frowning as he remembered their wish to keep away from Mr. Bulke.

"Er," hesitated Uncle Bob.

"Why, Mr. Bulke—did you want to speak to us?" Thomasina gazed at him with studied interest.

"'Course I wanted to speak to you! Saw that storm coming, and tried to tell you. Didn't know then that you hadn't any oars, of course."

"You didn't know we hadn't any oars?" Hongi repeated slowly, "But we thought—"

"Hongi, do butter this bread," said Aunt Jenny pushing a loaf towards him, "or toast it, or—or something."

Mr. Bulke turned to Uncle Bob, "Always can tell when there's a storm coming. Sort of smell it, I think."

"That's right," Lan looked up eagerly. "I smell them, too, but I thought people would laugh if I said that."

"Well, if sailors can smell icebergs, I guess they can smell storms, also." Mr. Bulke sniffed appreciatively, "and talking about smells, this *kai*—"

"That's Maori for food," Thomasina explained, seeing Lan's puzzled expression.

"Learned it yesterday," Mr. Bulke smiled. "I know *wahine*, that's woman, and *whare*, that's house, and I guess I'll learn a lot more before I've finished. Like to settle in New Zealand, you know, when I retire from the sea."

Lan caught Hongi's glance.

To be on the spot for diamond smuggling? Lan's thoughts raced ahead. Yet no one, to look at Mr. Bulke sitting there, so quietly and so much at home could imagine it.

Aunt Jenny faced Mr. Bulke. "We find it difficult to put our thanks into words. You must realise that we'd have been swept out to sea, only you were brave enough to come to our rescue. And in that storm—"

"And after you had tried to warn us, and we took no notice," Uncle Bob's voice was very quiet.

Mr. Bulke waved aside their thanks, and shrugged his massive shoulders. "You'd have done as much for anyone," he said, standing up and helping Thomasina to lay the cloth on the table.

"I'll ring your home and ask if you may stay till the storm dies down," Aunt Jenny said to Thomasina. Thomasina smiled her thanks.

"Looks like the storm will last quite a bit." Mr. Bulke moved to the cupboard and set out pepper and salt.

"I'll do that." Thomasina took over, and set the table in record time.

Mr. Bulke lowered himself on to his chair again. Wuffit settled cosily on his shoes, and watched warily, lest the feet passing and repassing should stand on his tail.

A sudden rush of wind tore at the house. Wuffit whined on a thin, high, piercing note.

"He doesn't like the storm," Thomasina paused. "He's afraid of something."

So are we, Lan thought. All of us, except Mr. Bulke. He suddenly felt tired and apprehensive.

Potatoes fried in the pan with a sizzling protest.

In the room the food smells were warm and comforting. Outside the rain pelted on the windows and on the corrugated iron roof. The wind again shrieked like some creature in torment, and rushed screaming round the house as if seeking something, endlessly and fruit-lessly.

"Tomato soup?" Aunt Jenny's voice broke the spell.

"I don't think I've ever tasted food as wonderful as this," said Hongi then he put down his knife and fork.

"It was only tomato soup, and fried bacon and potatoes, and tea." Aunt Jenny shrugged disparagingly.

"I know what Hongi means," Thomasina agreed and looked at them all. "It was food in warmth and shelter with the storm howling outside—"

"It was food in safety after we had been terrified on the sea," Lan looked at Mr. Bulke. "Thank you, sir." His eyes held steady, but his mind raced on. What's his game? Why did they kidnap us and take us to Te Mata Peak, and then when one of them has the chance to let us drift out to sea in a storm he risks his own life to rescue us?

After Mr. Bulke had left, followed by their repeated thanks, Uncle Bob took Thomasina home.

Lan, with puzzled eyes, turned to Hongi. Hongi wrinkled his forehead and raised his hands, palms up-wards. "I can't make it out, Lan," he said, as the door opened and Uncle Bob, shaking the rain from his hat and coat, came in out of the storm.

"I can't make it out, either," Uncle Bob muttered, spreading his coat to dry on the back of a chair.

In his bed that night Lan lay awake for a long time, listening to the wind and the rain beating against the house, and the trees, dark shadows in the garden, tossing and writhing, creaking and grumbling. He sat up and looked through the window at the driving rain.

It looks as if the whole sky's falling, he thought.

At last he fell asleep and slept dreamlessly until morning.

A pale and apologetic sun speared between the curtains and rested on Lan's pillow. He yawned lazily and turned over.

"You're awake at last," Hongi's voice growled in his ear.

"Not!" Lan muttered, and covered up his head with a sheet to shut out the day.

Wuffit's claws scraped on the floor.

Wuffit leaped and fell, and tried again. With a scrabble and a tug he reached the mound that was Lan under the bedclothes, and walked in many suspicious circles before he settled, heavily and contentedly, on top.

Lan opened one eye. "Go away!" he said, briefly, before he shut it again.

Nobody moved. Wuffit settled more heavily. His tail thumped with evident and rhythmical pleasure.

"Get off, you walloping lump!" Lan roared at him, suddenly sitting up, and heaving with his knees until Wuffit, dislodged from his hillock, avalanched down from the bed, and scrabbled through the doorway.

"How's the storm?" Lan rubbed his eyes, and stretched as he yawned widely.

Hongi pulled the blind up higher, and peered into the garden.

"All gone," he announced. "Sun's out."

The sun had already found Lan's head, and was warmng it pleasantly.

"There's quite a wind," Hongi said. "I went out to the gate to bring in the milk, and two of the bottles had blown over. Weren't broken, though. But the storm's gone."

"Could we do some swimming, then?" Lan collected his clothes from the floor, where Wuffit had scattered them in his scurryings.

"We sure could, but I tell you what. Let's get Thomasina to show us the rock pools, and tell us a bit about them. She'll be along after breakfast."

"I think I heard about Thomasina and the rock pools before, in Napier. She doesn't bother tracking you down when she can watch sea creatures and seaweed, wasn't that it?"

"Too right." Grinning, Hongi rubbed his left foot on his right ankle in a familiar movement.

"I'd still like to go back to Napier, and see what we could

find out. I feel we just had our hands on something, if we only knew what it was," Lan said over his shoulder, an he left for the bathroom.

"There's a lot we could find out, if we had half a chance," Hongi raised his voice, as Lan passed out of sight.

"What could you find out?" Uncle Bob put his head round the door.

"Just our detective work," Hongi grinned, his teeth showing white against his brown face. "In Napier, I mean."

"I've been giving it a bit of thought," Uncle Bob paused. "I'm not sure that we should stay here. I'm very grateful to Bulke for rescuing us, but I suppose that by now our whereabouts are no secret. His friends, and especially the one who owns the blue car, must be greatly interested in us. I'll discuss it later with Aunt Jenny and see what she thinks."

"I know I've heard there's a playground here. Isn't there, Hongi?" Aunt Jenny asked as she piled his plate with yellow peaches and ready prepared wheat cereal.

"Yes, Mrs. Sherwood, there's quite a big one."

"Oh, call me Aunt Jenny as the others do, Hongi."

"And I'm Uncle Bob, not Mr. Sherwood."

Hongi laughed. "It'll be easier that way. Oh, yes, the playground. Slides and swings and swingboats and things like that. But if we kept in sight could we climb a bit, and also explore the rock pools? Thomasina is interested in them, and they should be quite something after the storm."

"Yes, keep in sight," Uncle Bob boomed, swallowing a

mouthful of hot tea hastily. "I don't know what's behind this kidnapping in Napier, so I'm still suspicious of those men—and of any of their friends."

"The rock pools are decided on then." Lan buttered another piece of bread. "Do you realise I'm eating what's known in England as 'wonderful New Zealand butter'?" He waved his buttery knife to emphasise it. "And on its native heath, too."

Rat-a-tat! A mighty bang sounded on the kitchen door. Thomasina's warm red head appeared as she opened it from outside. "Anyone home?" she asked, unnecessarily. Her long legs, clad in faded green shorts, edged round the door. A T-shirted top followed.

"Come in, Thomasina," Aunt Jenny smiled. "They'd like you to show them some of the pools. But no rowing out to Tapu-te-Ranga."

"We wouldn't want to after yesterday, though Hongi and I have often done it," Thomasina assured her. "But the pools! I found a real humdinger this morning. It had oodles of things in it." Thomasina, with practised hands, began to clear the table. "Limpets and chitons and hermit crabs and periwinkles—"

"Stop! Stop!" Lan begged her, pretending to aim a plate at her head, and then suddenly adding it to the pile in front of her. "Don't you realise I'm a tenderfoot from one of the hugest cities in the world? And those things just don't grow or swim on London streets. I've never seen half of them."

"Gosh!" breathed Thomasina. "Haven't you ever? Not really?"

"Really and truly," Lan assured her. "Of course I've seen little things like Big Ben and the Tower where the princes were locked up, and Buckingham Palace, and the Thames, and—"

"All right. You win," Thomasina laughed. "I'd love to see London, and lots of other places, too. But for sheer magic it's hard to beat the sea after a storm, and the busy sea-creature world that lives beside it and in it."

"You're in sight of the house right along the beach," Uncle Bob grunted. "Just keep where I can see you if I put my head over the fence. You'll be home for lunch?"

"Too right!" Hongi gave a half leap and raced for the gate. Wuffit reached it a split second in front of him.

The morning smelled damp and salty, and the island lay dark brown, surrounded by jagged rocks. The wind had ceased its wailing, but a steady breeze blew straight from the south, from the Antarctic. The sun hid for a few moments behind a racing cloud before it burst forth triumphantly.

"Whoops!" shouted Hongi.

"Smashing!" Lan leaped from the concrete wall above the beach on to the sand.

"Wuff!" barked Wuffit at a seagull.

The wet sand was firm beneath their feet, and Lan and Hongi raced wildly to the ragged brown rocks. Wuffit scampered somewhere between their flying feet. Thomasina followed.

"That's a pipi," said Thomasina peering at a shell Lan was now cradling in his hand. "Maoris like to eat pipis, and you often find lots of pipi shells in heaps."

"What's that white bird like a little seagull?" Lan asked as Thomasina came towards the rock pools. His eyes were screwed up against the sun as he watched.

"It's a tern."

Hongi glanced at the tern, and then turned his dark head towards a small pool in the rocks. "Here's a periwinkle. Lots of periwinkles, in fact." He gazed at the little bluish-white spiral shells.

"And limpets," Thomasina pointed out a greyish-green shell clamped to a rock.

"Chitons!" Hongi moved closer to the pool.

"Just like limpets," said Lan and tried to push one off its rock.

"They're not, you know, Lan," Thomasina paused. "Chitons have eight movable pieces on their shell. See!"

"There's a hermit crab!" Thomasina bent lower. "See that little shell walking, Lan? That's a borrowed shell, with friend crab inside. Shrewd, isn't he?"

"Too right!" Hongi agreed.

"Little claws, walking along." Lan then turned to put one finger on a sea-anemone. Promptly the tentacles closed round it.

Hongi pulled out a vivid green piece of seaweed. "Here's sea lettuce, just like real lettuce, and those brown bead-like things are called Neptune's necklace. The blobs of red jelly are trying to fool you. They're really red sea-anemones contracted or folded up."

"I've learned more this morning than I'd learn in a day at school," Lan grinned. "But I don't think I can absorb too much at the one time. I want to remember it all." He glanced over the pool again, naming the types of shell and seaweed. "Yes, I think I can remember them all." One finger drew their shapes in the air as he thought.

They were all silent for a few moments while Lan studied the sky, and the swooping terns, and the seagulls in search of food. One came and looked at them with glassy eyes and held an inquiring head on one side.

"Let's look at the fishing boats and the nets," suggested Lan standing up.

They strolled away from the rock pools past their house, and waved to Uncle Bob who was oiling the hinges on the front gate.

"Lobster pots," Lan said as they came to piled-up lobster baskets drying in the sun.

"Fishing nets." Hongi peeped through the open weave of one, and touched one of the large cork floats.

"Race you to the top of that rock!" Lan laughed suddenly at Hongi, and turning, sped away back in the direction from which they had come.

"Look! Look!" Some children with the dark eyes and hair of Italians laughed as they watched. They clapped their hands as Hongi reached Lan and outstripped him. Thomasina stood, with the freshening breeze blowing her hair, and her hands shading her eyes.

"Hongi'll get there first." Thomasina looked at them before she bent to pick up a huge irridescent shell. Then, half to herself, "No, Lan's winning! Gosh, he'd better be careful on those rocks. You can easily—"

Even from where she stood she could hear Lan's sharp cry as he threw up his arms, and fell in a crumpled heap on the rocks.

Before she reached him Lan was standing on one foot, clutching on to a jagged piece of stone. He stood perfectly still, the colour drained from his face.

"I'm afraid," he said, rather jerkily, "that I've sprained my ankle or something. I can't walk on it."

With a wry grimace he sat down suddenly. "First my arm, and when that gets better I have to do this!"

"What rotten luck," Hongi frowned in sympathy. He beckoned urgently to Uncle Bob, who was crossing the road with swift, anxious strides.

Uncle Bob took in the situation with one glance from under his beetling eyebrows. He knelt, and with surprisingly gentle, large fingers explored Lan's ankle.

"It's not broken. At least I don't think so. Chair!" He grasped his own wrist with one hand, and Hongi's with the other. "Now, gently does it, Lan. Just ease on to this seat, and we'll get you home in no time."

"I wish I could help," Thomasina, walking with dragging feet, sounded wistful.

"Well, run home and warn Aunt Jenny. She might get a real fright if she saw Lan had to be carried home like this."

Wuffit walked sadly beside them, his tail between his legs, as if he had done something disgraceful.

"Cheer up, Wuffit! Not your fault, old man. There, good dog! Wuffit, stop jumping up! Someone'll trip over you in a minute," and Uncle Bob waved one leg to shoo him off.

"Wuff! Wuff!" and Wuffit turned a sort of spiral in the air, from sheer exuberance.

"Well, Lan Sherwood, imagine doing a silly thing like spraining your ankle on a holiday!" Aunt Jenny greeted him with anxious, scolding surprise.

"Sounds as if a holiday were a sharp piece of rock, suitable for spraining ankles, of course," Uncle Bob teased her.

He and Hongi lowered Lan into the old armchair by the kitchen window.

"I'll ring the doctor. Who is a good doctor, Thomasina?" Uncle Bob looked over his shoulder.

"She's 'phoned the doctor already," Aunt Jenny was gently easing off Lan's sandal.

"Ouch!" Lan grimaced as he gingerly put his foot to the ground.

"Well, this decides things," Uncle Bob said leaning against the doorway as he packed tobacco with staccato stabs into his pipe. "We might as well go back to Napier. I'll tell the police that Bulke found out we were here, and probably has told his friends. You can both lie low in Napier, and we won't advertise the fact that you are there, except to the police."

"Good." Lan smiled faintly, and wrinkled parallel lines across his forehead. "Both Hongi and I want to go on ferreting out things."

"No ferreting," Uncle Bob said with almost savage firmness. "I feel partly to blame for letting you get into that mess on Te Mata Peak. From now on you can stick stamps in albums, or do your knitting!"

"Wow!" Hongi grinned. "I can just see us!"

"I'll be left out!" Thomasina wailed. "I've got to stay in Island Bay now that I'm home."

"We'll write a full account of everything," Lan promised her. "We have to let the bishop know all about our adventures, and we'll do a carbon copy for you. It'll be something to do, I suppose, until I can walk on this ankle again."

"The *Golden Star* is still held up in Napier, because of the shipping strike, but she may be sailing any day." Uncle

Bob moved towards the telephone. "I'll ring and see whether I can get some seats on the 'plane." He left them sitting dejectedly while he crossed to the lounge.

The door bell rang imperatively.

Uncle Bob could hear Aunt Jenny's voice in the hall, "Through here, Doctor. Wasn't it fortunate that you could come so soon?" before the kitchen door closed on her words.

"I suppose it's very busy at this time of the year," Uncle Bob said into the telephone. "I'd be glad if you'd let me know of any cancellations. Thank you very much."

He strolled over to the window, and stood for a long time drumming his fingers on the window sill. He was roused from his thought by the sound of Aunt Jenny's voice bidding the doctor good-bye and opening the front door.

"Feel better now, Lan?" Uncle Bob strode into the kitchen.

"Much better, but I've got to rest this for a week." Lan indicated the firm bandages on his ankle. "Thomasina gave me this shell to cheer me up."

"My word, it's a beauty, Thomasina," Uncle Bob said admiringly.

"Sure you don't want to keep it yourself?" Lan gazed at the opalescent blues and greens with flashes of fire. "It's as big as my hand. It's a beauty. What's it called, Thomasina?"

"Paua. The holes in that row are for letting out water. And I'll get lots for you. I know where to find them. Lots of people eat pauas. You have to bang them with a hammer, and cover them with flour or batter, and grill them for just three minutes," Thomasina said.

"Can you eat the whole fish?" Aunt Jenny appeared in time to hear Thomasina's words.

"Oh, no. You throw away all the soft parts, and the white with the tiny, sharp teeth," Hongi said.

"Bob," Aunt Jenny lowered her voice, "Mr. Bulke was coming up the path as I opened the door for the doctor. He's in the lounge now."

"Who, the doctor?"

"No, Mr. Bulke, silly! He says there's a storm coming. A bad one. He can smell it in the air."

"I'll go and talk to him. Will you put on the kettle?"

Mr. Bulke was putting down the telephone receiver as Uncle Bob entered.

"Sorry to answer your 'phone, Sherwood, but no one else seemed to hear, and I'd picked it up from sheer force of habit before I remembered that I wasn't in my own house."

Uncle Bob waited.

"It was the airways. The girl didn't think there was a hope of a booking in the next few days. Some of the airports down south have been closed, because of a storm from the Antarctic. Wouldn't expect it in the middle of summer, would you?"

"You would not," Uncle Bob agreed tersely.

"Might be waiting for days, or have to go by bus or something." Mr. Bulke shifted to a more comfortable position in his chair. His eyes seemed small, set in his large, square face. "I'll be going back to Napier to-morrow. Only too delighted to take you all along with me. How about it, Sherwood?"

"Thank you very much," Uncle Bob said, heavily.

CHAPTER FIFTEEN

TRAPPED

"IT'S TOUGH on you having to stay at home," said Aunt Jenny as she paused at the headquarters of the Junior C.I.B. Her eyes crinkled at the edges as she smiled: "But good of Mr. Bulke to bring us all back safely."

Lan and Hongi looked up from the saw bench, where they were busy hammering.

"Bonzer," Hongi agreed, "but poor Thomasina was as mopey as a wet hen when she had to stay behind."

"She may be able to come back to Napier when the strike is over, and the *Golden Star* has gone. I've asked her to stay with us, anyway," Aunt Jenny said. "But I'm sure you don't like being at home all the time."

"We don't mind," Hongi assured her. "And as the police ordered us to stay here until the *Golden Star* sails to-morrow, we haven't any choice."

Lan silently indicated his injured ankle.

"Well, of course, you couldn't have gone very far with that ankle, Lan, but—"

"It's your cooking that's keeping us at home, Aunt Jenny," Hongi assured her.

Aunt Jenny laughed. "Go on with you, Hongi! Flatterers, that's what you are! But I'll see if I can turn on something extra special." Still laughing, she turned back towards the house.

"It shouldn't be long now, Senior Detective Lan."

Hongi nailed another piece of wood in position on the aeroplane he was making. "The police should nab them soon. They'll have to hurry though, if the *Golden Star* sails to-morrow."

"I certainly hope so. They got the Pania statuette back on the stall without being seen?"

"Too right. A real sleight-of-hand. Gosh, this waiting gets harder all the time." Hongi hammered vigorously. "I'm glad your uncle was able to get back my fishing rod from Bluff Hill. I'm sort of attached to that rod."

Lan laughed. He stood tall and thin on one foot, resting the sprained one, while the fingers of one hand began to tap restlessly. "This waiting!" He picked up a saw, and set to work, shaping the deck of a boat.

Uncle Bob ambled round the side of the house. "Just look at Uncle," Lan grinned, "ambling about. I've never seen him walk like that before. Usually he has a quick, determined sort of stride. I suppose the waiting is worrying him, too."

The telephone began to ring in the distance. Lan looked at Hongi. Hongi looked at Lan. "Perhaps this is it," Lan muttered, with the saw held suspended in mid-air.

"Are you there?" Aunt Jenny called from the back porch. Lan and Hongi stared anxiously towards the door. Uncle Bob was striding purposefully towards the house.

"It's the man from the garage," Aunt Jenny laughed at their anxiety. "He says the re-bore on our car is finished at last, and we can collect it any time we like."

With tight lips Lan groaned and sighed deeply, the sigh of one whose patience has been tried too far. He shrugged and went back to his sawing.

"I was sort of getting accustomed to the Rolls-Noise." Hongi gazed sentimentally at the licence number 131313. "It's much more exciting than a modern car. You can keep your streamlined beauties," he said generously. "Give me a rattling old girl with asthma."

"We'll have the Rolls-Noise for a few more days. Its owner is away on holiday," Uncle Bob called.

"Aunt Jenny has some shopping to do in town, boys. I'll just run her in, and I'll be right back." Uncle Bob put his head round the door of the C.I.B. Junior Headquarters. "I won't be very long. Just stay in the garden or the house and keep an ear out for the 'phone. The police check up every little while." He strode to the Rolls-Noise, and Lan and Hongi listened to the splutters and coughs that were the usual preliminaries of a Rolls-Noise journey.

Lan, with careful concentration, had just planed off a curl of yellow wood, when the telephone bell rang.

"You go, Hongi," he said. "My ankle makes me a bit slow." He put down the plane, and followed Hongi to the house. As Lan entered Hongi was hanging up the telephone receiver.

"The police were surprised that your uncle and your aunt weren't here. They're sending some plain clothes men to pick us up. They want to check up on some details. They knew about your ankle, Lan, and said we'd need a car. We'll bring our notes, too. They'll meet us at the gate in five minutes."

"I'll leave a note for Aunt and Uncle to tell them we're at the police station." Lan limped over to the house, and scribbled industriously. He left the note in the middle of the kitchen table, and carefully weighed it down with a biscuit tin. "They're bound to find it here."

The two boys folded their smuggling notes carefully, and stowed them in their pockets. In five minutes they reached the garden gate just as a dark car slid to a halt. There were two men inside. The one next to the driver leaned round and opened the back door for the boys. The door slammed after them.

They were travelling fast and silently. Lan turned to Hongi, "Bit different from the Rolls-Noise!"

"It's a real rumpty dooler," Hongi grinned.

Now the car was mounting steadily.

"Here!" Hongi's voice held alarm. "This isn't the way to the police station."

"No, it's not. Just a little matter we wanted to fix up first," the driver grunted.

Lan looked at him carefully for the first time. He could see the man's eyes, blue and metallic, in the rear vision mirror. The back of his neck bulged over his collar, and at the brown hair line a small mole nestled into a crease of flesh. A sudden thrill of fear shot through the boy. The other man, thin, muffled in spite of the heat, wore a hat pulled down over his eyes. He was speaking, easily, calmly, in a high, lingering sort of drawl.

"We just want to see if you can identify some equipment the police keep up here in a shed. Won't be long now."

The car turned in at a private driveway, passed an old house painted red, and slid to a halt.

"Here we are. The shed's over there," the driver said, as he and the thin man walked slowly, one on each side of the boys. "See if you can give us some clues from the equipment in there."

The shed door was thrown open, and the car driver

followed Hongi and the limping Lan as they stepped into the damp-smelling semi-darkness. The door was shut and bolted hastily.

"What the—?" Lan demanded.

"I say, cut it out!" Hongi protested.

"Drop everything in your pockets on to the floor," the driver ordered. He glanced at the heap at Lan's feet—a peach stone, one nib, a handkerchief, a pocket-knife, paper and a stub of pencil—and at the contents of Hongi's pockets—chewing gum, handkerchief, pocket-knife, a round stone and some sheets of seemingly blank paper.

"Here, you," he nodded to Lan, "no funny business, mind. Just pick up those pocket-knives, the nib and the stone and bring them to me. You can put the rest back in your pockets."

Quietly Lan did as he was told, and limped over to give them to the man, who backed to the door. Without turning, he stretched his hand behind him, and knocked twice. The bolt flew back and the man edged out.

"You can yell your heads off," the thin man's voice called through the door when it was locked again. "No one will hear you in a month of Sundays." He laughed derisively, and Lan knew where he had heard that squeaky laugh before. In panic his mind flashed back to the *Golden Star*, and to the bald-headed captain and the thin, rat-like man on the wharf. Again he could hear "The Roundabout".

"We're trapped!" Hongi looked at Lan in the half-gloom. "We fell for their corny bait, hook, line and sinker. Of all the bucket-brained—!"

"Yes," Lan agreed slowly. "Uncle said not to run into

any danger, and here we are! He'll think we're at the police station when he reads my note, and he won't look for us. Not that he'd think of looking up here even if he were searching for us."

They could hear the men talking in low tones outside, and strained to hear the words.

"We'll signal them, and get the stuff out at about ten to-night," the rat-like, squeaky voice said softly. "That'll be the last lot."

"What about the boys?" the other voice asked. "Don't forget they've seen us, and they know too much to be safe."

"You don't have to worry about them," the rat voice replied. "Sure they've seen us. Sure they know what the game is—or some of it any way—but what's the fuss about? We'll take them for a nice little sail after dark. They won't have much chance to spill the beans after that." The voices died away, as the men moved out of earshot.

"They—they're going to drown us!" Lan's voice was quiet with fear.

"Yes," Hongi gulped on the word, and was silent.

"We've got to get out. We've just got to," Lan whispered. Hongi said nothing. He seemed deep in thought.

"They haven't bound us," he said, at length. "They must be quite sure we can't get out of here."

"It seems like it," said Lan trying to keep the despair out of his voice.

They looked round the shed. Their eyes were getting accustomed to the half-light, but there was little to see. Not a single object lay on the dusty wooden floor, nothing but cobwebs decorated the unlined walls. There was one tiny, dirty window, barely ten inches square.

"Well, we couldn't get out of this." Hongi rubbed his hand over the glass to clear it.

Lan looked out. "Nothing but a few bushes, and a grassy hillside," he muttered.

Hongi tried the door. It remained solid and firm.

"I've heard of people opening doors by slipping a piece of paper under them, and pushing the key out of the lock—"

"And then drawing in the paper, and hey presto, there's the key," Lan interrupted. "Only thing is, that though we have paper the gap under the door is so small that I doubt if a piece of paper could be slipped out, much less a key pulled in." They lapsed into gloomy silence.

"Anyhow, there isn't a key, just a huge bolt on the outside." Hongi gazed at the door. "Even the hinges are on the outside. I did think of unscrewing the lock with my pocket-knife, only there isn't a lock," he shrugged, "and they've taken our pocket-knives," he remembered.

"What I'd give to see Thomasina and the bishop now," and Lan stared at the dusty floor.

"There's a spider up there in the corner," Hongi said, gloomily. "Usually I'm interested in spiders, but not to-day, somehow." He went on gazing at it unseeingly as he thought aloud. "I once heard of some children climbing out of an old-fashioned chimney," he said, at length.

"Trouble is there isn't a chimney, old-fashioned or otherwise," Lan groaned. "There isn't anything. No garden tools, no axe, nothing. Not even a box to sit on. No secret springs opening doors into winding passages, no barred windows and rusty files, just waiting to saw us out. Nothing, except one enormous spider."

"And a lot of dust," Hongi added, gloomily. "They haven't left a guard, by the sound of things—or the lack of sound," he added. "Anyhow, the shed door faces the house, so I suppose they'd see us if we tried to get out that way."

"They know we don't need a guard. We just couldn't get out of this in a hundred years." Lan crossed painfully to the window, and stood gloomily gazing out. Then he limped back to where his belongings lay on the floor, and stuffed them impatiently into his pockets.

The minutes ticked slowly by. Lan glanced at his watch. "Half past one," he muttered. "They'll be having lunch at home."

"I don't feel hungry," Hongi said licking dry lips, "but I could do with a drink, all right. Nothing like being scared for making you feel parched."

"I'm pretty scared myself," Lan admitted, his forehead wrinkled in thought. He sat down on the floor, and rubbed his swollen ankle gently.

Hongi continued to gaze at the fawn stripes of the spider. He admired its black velvet appearance. Then he, too, sat on the floor.

"I have an idea," Lan hesitated. Hongi turned quickly. "Well," Lan went on slowly, "you know how weatherboards are nailed on from the outside? Perhaps if we pushed these, we could loosen them enough to push out some boards."

"It's worth trying. I'll do the higher bits, and you do the lower, because of your foot." Hongi climbed up the dwangs between the studs.

"Thanks," Lan scrambled to his feet. "I'd find it a

bit difficult getting up on those cross-pieces between the posts." He watched Hongi thumping systematically along the rough-hewn wall boards.

"Nothing loose here," his voice showed his disappointment, as he climbed down.

"No good here, either," Lan said, at length. His shoulders drooped. He sat on the floor thinking and thinking, while Hongi stood looking at the spider.

"I wonder," Lan gazed at the ceiling, "if we could force up the corrugated iron on the roof, enough to make a hole big enough for us to get out."

"We could try," Hongi said, softly, "but the trouble is they might hear us. They're probably in the house we passed when we turned into the driveway. They'd know not to take any notice of shouting, but iron wrenching off from a roof is not exactly a silent job. And they could see us getting out. We'll try, though."

He climbed on the supporting beams until he was within reach of the ceiling. Hongi pushed as hard as he could. The iron remained firm.

"It's probably got a board holding it down round the edges," he gasped at length. "I can't make any impression on it. They'd hear a noise like bending iron, anyway, and come at the double."

"I'll have a go at it, if you give me a hand," Lan stood up. "I'm not too good at climbing with this ankle." He rested his arm on Hongi's shoulder, and heaved himself up, climbing on the dwangs until he could reach the roofing sheets.

"It's no good," he said. "I can't move it an inch." Painfully he climbed down, and took up his position on the floor.

"Draughty here," he muttered. "The wind seems to come up between the floorboards."

"Probably the shed is on piles." Hongi gave his attention to the spider. "Then the wind would come in through the cracks between the floorboards." He jumped up suddenly to see the spider, slipped and crashed down on to the floor. His foot disappeared through a wet, rotten floorboard.

Hongi opened his mouth, and shut it again.

Silently Lan was at his side, tugging at Hongi's foot. Hongi manoeuvred it up through the floorboard. His sandal and part of his leg were covered with wet, dank-smelling mud.

"There's a spring there. Under the shed," Hongi gasped, in his excitement. "There often are hidden springs on the hills."

"Or it might be a broken drain pipe," Lan suggested.

Eagerly they cracked away another piece of wood.

"Quietly, now," Lan whispered. "Not a sound in case they come back." Daylight streamed through the widening hole. "Look, Hongi, the shed's probably on piles, just like you said. If we could make a big enough hole we might be able to get out."

Hongi lay on the floor, and tried to peer sideways through the hole, "I can't quite see yet," he confessed, "but there's a terrific draught, so I'm sure the shed must be on piles at the back—quite high piles at the far side where the hill slopes down."

They wrenched a three-inch nail out of the rotten joist underneath, and chipped away at the wood diligently.

Lan stiffened.

"Ssh! They're coming!" he gasped, pushing the splintered wood into the hole.

The heavy bolt shot back and a shadow fell in the inched-open doorway. "Here's a bit of grub for you boys," and the driver of the car glanced sharply at them—at Hongi coming for the food, and at Lan crouched on the floor in the far corner of the gloomy shed. The bolt shot home before Hongi reached the door.

"He's careful to shut the door quickly in case we attack him," Hongi muttered.

Lan wiped the gathering sweat of fear from his forehead.

"Gosh!" he gasped. "That sure put the wind up on me."

"Me, too," Hongi agreed, as they set to work again.

"Suspicious blokes," Lan said, glancing at the bowl. "They didn't even give us spoons."

The food, a sort of stew, remained untouched in its bowl near the door.

"Here's another nail." Lan pushed it back and forth to ease it out of the rotting joist under the floorboards. "We'll pull away as much rotten wood as we can, and then chip away with the nails to get a hole big enough to crawl out. It'll take hours and hours," he added, as he pulled out a small, chunky piece of wood.

"Perhaps we'd better pour the stew down the hole," Hongi suggested. "Don't want to make them angry, as I'm sure they would be if we just left it."

Lan limped over to the bowl, and glanced out through the window as he passed it. "The signal! They're using the signal, even though it's daylight. It must be one of those hooded Aldis lamps, and they must be just above here. I wish we could tell Uncle where they're signalling from. He thought it would be Bluff Hill."

"It is still Bluff Hill, but round a bit," said Hongi as he joined Lan at the window. "I didn't see the names of the streets we came up, but it is part of Bluff Hill."

"Yes," Lan agreed, "though there wasn't that particularly strong smell of flowers." He emptied the stew down the hole, on to the seeping ground below. "That sort of signalling lamp was in the back of the blue car—the one Mr. Bulke was driving, and that watch case with the marks was in his cabin. Perhaps he—" Lan said, thoughtfully.

"Yet he risked his life to save us, and he brought us safely back to Napier. I don't get it at all." Hongi put the bowl back carefully by the door.

"It'll be a bit of a squeeze crawling under. We're not very high up from the ground here," Lan pondered aloud.

"It seems to slope away more steeply at the other side," Hongi observed chipping away diligently with his nail.

"It wasn't so bad the first half hour, but now I feel as if I have nails in my bones." Lan let out a deep breath, and gently rubbed the blisters on his hands.

"We've been at it for hours. What's the time now?"

"You ask every ten minutes," Lan grinned, tiredly. "It's half-past six."

"The hole's almost big enough," Hongi tested it carefully, "though my shoulders are too wide."

"They might bring us more food. Better put our shirts over the gap, and I'll sit in front of it, if we hear them coming."

For a long half hour they chipped and pushed at firmer wood.

"I can hear them!" Hongi's shirt was tossed over the hole, and Lan's rested carelessly beside it. Lan nursed his swollen ankle as he sat, a dejected figure on the floor.

The bolt shot back. The empty bowl was silently replaced by another bowl of stew. The door was shut again before Hongi reached it. The boys waited breathlessly until the footsteps died away.

Sweat poured from their foreheads, as they pushed the nails into the wood, and chipped it away bit by tiny bit. Another hour passed.

"We'd better put on our shirts now." Lan eased his ankle into a more comfortable position. "We've nearly finished."

"They won't be able to see us from the house, because of the slope of the hill, and the door will be bolted. We didn't make a sound, so we ought to have a good chance of escaping without being seen. They mightn't find out for hours," Hongi whispered, cheerfully.

"If it weren't for my ankle," Lan groaned, "we'd have a much better chance."

"We'll stick together." Hongi's mouth was determined.

"It'll take us quite a while to get home," said Lan as he stood up carefully.

"Home?" Hongi's teeth gleamed. "That's the first route they'd take if they found out we'd escaped. No, Lan, we'll go to the Mardi Gras, and try to catch them red-handed. They'll be getting rid of the last haul at ten o'clock, they said."

"If they go free they might kidnap or drown other people—people like Thomasina, perhaps." Lan's breath came in little gasps. His grey eyes were like steel. "We'll go to the Mardi Gras."

CHAPTER SIXTEEN

THOMASINA SAT in the early morning sun on the Island Bay sea wall. Her legs dangled above the dry, heaped-up sand, and beat an angry tattoo on the side of the wall. Her camera hung limply at her side, and her fingers crunched a handful of shells in a vain effort to calm her feelings.

"If only I could have gone back to Napier with Hongi and Lan," she muttered, her face becoming redder and redder as she became angrier and angrier. "Lan's Aunt Jenny asked me to stay. I wouldn't have moved an inch away from their house until the *Golden Star* sailed. But you couldn't convince Mum of a thing like that," and she kicked the wall all the harder as she remembered the scene with her mother the day before, when the Sherwoods and Hongi had left Island Bay.

A group of Maoris, a middle-aged couple and their grown-up son and their daughter were passing. She had seen them before. The mother was big and loosely dressed, as if she had shrunk a little, but her clothes had remained large, ready for her to grow again. Her son carried a gleaming kitchen knife. Her husband swung an empty sugar sack as he walked. He was darker than his wife, but looked absurdly like her in too big clothes. The daughter's gaily coloured skirt swung lazily as she walked.

Their voices, low and blurred, carried to Thomasina. She strained her ears.

"Wonder if they're talking in Maori or in English?" she pondered. As her anger cooled the colour in her face began to fade to a raw sunburnt pink.

The Maoris were nearly past. "Goin' to get pauas," the daughter called to her. " You know where there's a good place?"

"Yes. Yes, I do." Thomasina jumped from the wall. The sand was soft beneath her feet as she hurried to keep up. Now the sand was damp and firm as they approached the shingle. She glanced towards Tapu-te-Ranga, and watched the waves breaking on the jagged rocks. A group of climbers had reached the top of its rocky heights, and were waving happily. Thomasina waved in return, but she could not feel happy. "Here's the place," she said to the older woman.

"Very good place," her new friend smiled. "Get lots of pauas here." She followed Thomasina with heavy steps over the sharp, brown rocks where they jutted into the sea.

Thomasina hesitated. The kitchen knife gleamed in the young Maori's hand. He stepped to the edge of the rocks and leaned over.

"Here's a littley," he said, and bent down into the water, hacking with his knife. His sister, pressing nearer to see, lost her footing and fell with a sudden splash into the water.

"Not much good that, eh?" she laughed with the others, as she struggled out, and sat on a rock to dry. She continued to laugh, her brown face fat, jolly and easy. Thomasina felt the last of her anger evaporate, as she bent to peer under the loose rocks.

The young man with the knife stepped, fully clothed,

into the water, and with a determined effort, silently
prised off the shellfish from the rocks. He tossed every
new one to his sister, who dropped them inside the sag-
ging sack. It began to have shape in the bottom, and
Thomasina ran back a short way, and aimed her camera
at the group.

"Now, none of that," chuckled the Maori in the sea,
"Put the pauas off, having their photos taken."

"And you'll break the camera," the girl with the sack
teased him.

"Take a picture of her instead." His white teeth gleamed
in his brown face. "That'll fix your camera good-o."

His sister hid her face in the sugar bag, and shrieks of
muffled laughter could be heard.

"Big paua!" the young man called, and held up an
empty hand. "That got her out!" he called to Thomasina,
as the girl opened the bag, and held out her hand. Thomasina laughed, and in a split second had clicked the
shutter.

A shadow fell on Thomasina, and she wheeled round.

"Well," she said, as she recognised the round figure in
black gaiters, and the uncovered bald head of the bishop,
"I didn't expect to see you taking photos here."

"Of course I'm here." the bishop's camera aimed
at Thomasina and the young man sprawling in the
water, bending to uncover a rock. "I said I'd come here
with my camera when you told me about it. Remember?"

"I do now, but I thought you'd have big important
things to do, like meetings, and dinners and sermons,"
Thomasina explained.

"Could anything be bigger or more important than

seeing the wonders of creation?" the bishop asked balancing precariously near the sea as he levelled his camera.

"No, I suppose not," Thomasina admitted, "and I'm very glad you came. The pools are particularly interesting after the storm. We expected another storm from the Antarctic," she added politely, "but it seems to have blown off somewhere else."

"Now where are your friends, Hongi and Lan? Surely they enjoy playing on the seashore, too?"

"Yes, they do, but they can't come now because yesterday they went back to Napier in the blue car—the one Mr. Bulke borrowed."

"Mr. Sherwood rang me about that, but he was not sure when they were going. And in Mr. Bulke's car," the bishop said softly, as if to himself. "Of course, Mr. Sherwood told me how you were all rescued, and how brave Mr. Bulke was. But in Mr. Bulke's car. The blue car. Well! Well!"

Thomasina shivered, as if a cloud had passed over the sun.

"It actually belongs to a friend of his," she said so that only the bishop could hear. "I think that the sight of that blue car on Te Mata Peak is painted like a picture somewhere inside me. It even comes to frighten me in the night. I don't know how Hongi and Lan could ever get into it again."

"Perhaps they had no choice," the bishop suggested slowly.

"No," Thomasina agreed. "Mr. Sherwood fixed it up. They had no choice." She stubbed her sandalled feet against the rocks, and said more loudly, "I do wish I could have gone back to Napier. Mrs. Sherwood asked me to stay with them, but Mum said I couldn't go while the strike was on."

"That the wharf strike?" the Maori mother asked.

Thomasina nodded.

"You were just too late," the bishop commented, "or perhaps I should say early."

"They fixed that late last night. Papers were full of it," explained her husband hitching up his trousers.

"And Mum didn't say a thing," Thomasina complained disgustedly.

"Well, I suppose she knew it would add to your disappointment if you knew about it. After all it was too late for you to go."

"Yes, you're right. She couldn't have done much about it. She doesn't like me travelling alone, so I couldn't go by bus or train," Thomasina shrugged resignedly.

The bishop appeared to be lost in thought.

"Havin' a good little serious talk, eh?" the Maori mother teased Thomasina.

"Yes, we're still talking about the shipping strike being over."

"Those two lazy hunters got no excuse to go fishing now. Down to the wharf this afternoon, and earn plenty money for kai." They all laughed good-humouredly, and the young man scrambled up on the rocks.

"I'll see you again," Thomasina smiled at the Maoris. "I hope you find lots of fish."

"And get plenty of kai," the bishop added kindly as he turned away with Thomasina.

"Are the boys writing that account of their adventures for me?" the bishop asked as they fell into step on the damp sand.

"Yes, sir, they are, and I'm helping, too. I'm doing the illustrations because I like drawing, and I've lots of photos, as well." Thomasina gave a small skip, but stopped immediately, remembering her elderly companion.

"Ah," the bishop smiled benignly, "I'll be most interested to see it. I'd better say good-bye to you, Thomasina, because I'll be returning north this afternoon. An ecclesiastical friend will accompany me as far as Hastings, and do most of the driving."

"You're going north?" Thomasina turned glowing eyes on him. "You wouldn't be going through Napier, after you left your friend at Hastings, would you? Oh, I'm sorry! I shouldn't have said that." Thomasina's face burned with embarrassment.

"Why, yes, I could easily go through Napier. If your mother were willing to let you come I'd be only too pleased," the bishop said kindly. "In fact, she might like to be with you."

"She can't because of minding my young brother," Thomasina explained panting with excitement, "and Dad's away on a job, so he can't help. But I'm sure she'd let me go, now that the strike's over, and now that I've someone who'll keep an eye on me—that's what she always says. Perhaps you'd come and ask her, sir. Then she'll know that I'm not making it all up, to get to Napier, you know. We live just along there," Thomasina waved a hand largely in the direction of the street.

"Certainly, that would be much the wisest," the bishop agreed, and they crossed the road together.

Thomasina walked slowly and carefully so that the bishop should in no way feel hurried. When you're as old as the bishop, she thought, curbing an almost over-whelming desire to skip and to shout in her excitement, you probably don't like being hustled.

They reached the house at length, and Thomasina, in honour of the occasion, led the bishop to the front door, and imperiously rang the bell.

"Oh, gee," she said, giving an uncontrollable half-skip, "I'm so excited. I never guessed anything like this would happen. Oh, it's wonderful! What time did you say you were leaving, sir?"

"Just after lunch, Thomasina. We'll be rather late arriving—we hadn't intended to go as far as Napier the first day—but we have to stop at Palmerston North for a while. I hope your mother won't mind if you're up a little later than usual. In fact we won't get there until midnight."

"Oh, no, I'm sure she won't," Thomasina assured him, not entirely truthfully. She gave another violent twist to the bell. "Funny she doesn't come. I'll just run round to the back, and see if she's there."

As he contemplated the daisies in the garden the bishop could hear footsteps approaching in the house.

The front door was opened quietly, and Thomasina, her eyes bright with unshed tears, stood before him, holding a sheet of scribbling-pad paper in her hand.

"Mum left the key for me, and she says to get my own lunch, as she'll be out till about afternoon tea time. She's gone shopping, so I don't know where to get her." Thomasina sniffed suddenly, and suddenly brushed the back of her hand roughly across her eyes. "Of all the rotten luck. Just when I had a chance of getting there."

"Perhaps it is all for the best," the bishop tried to console her.

"I don't believe it could be," Thomasina said, rebelliously, "but perhaps I'm better at home," she added with a deep sigh. "Would you like a cup of tea?" she smiled bleakly. "It's so kind of you to bother with me. Most people would be too busy, or too important," she said, with a revealing wisdom.

"Ah, no. Not tea now," the bishop said. "In my calling we almost suffer from an excess of tea."

A picture of the bishop trying to cope with an unending procession of cups of tea flashed into Thomasina's mind, and she smiled with him.

"I'm sorrier than I can say that you're so disappointed, Thomasina, but these things always turn out for the best, I've found in my long life. Thank you for the pieces of excitement that have brightened up my holiday. I shall be looking forward to seeing the account of your adventures. I'll be leaving Wellington at about two o'clock. Good-bye, Thomasina, I hope you have a very enjoyable holiday."

"I hope, sir, that you do, too." Thomasina stood with drooping shoulders, watching him go.

When he had passed out of sight she turned again into the house, and did not try to stop the tears spilling down her cheeks.

Her tongue felt swollen and dry, and she crossed to the kitchen sink to get a drink of water. The sink was piled high with dishes waiting to be washed. She went to her bedroom, and sat for a moment on the unmade bed.

"Wonder what's got into Mum," she muttered. "Not like her to go out and leave the house like this. She must be very tired." Thomasina hastily smoothed and made her bed.

The other beds were unmade, too. I'll just fix them up while I boil an egg for lunch, she thought, attacking them savagely, as if they were the cause of her disappointment.

The dishes in the kitchen sink turned unwashed faces to her in mute reproach.

"Gosh, Mum hasn't even taken the bits and pieces off," she muttered, busily scraping with a knife. She turned to find a piece of newspaper to wrap round the scraps. As she smoothed it out she began to read the "Personal Column". Her eyes were fixed on the first item.

"Well," she breathed, "so the bishop is staying at the Doncaster Hotel. Bet he never sees the dishes stacked up there." She banged the rubbish into the paper, opened the back door, and clanging the garbage tin lid in her anger, threw the rubbish parcel inside.

"There! I don't feel quite so savage," and she turned on the hot tap, and swooshed huge quantities of soap powder into the sink. " Wonder how Mum gets through all this three times a day, and then all the other things as well," she pondered, rubbing vigorously and then rinsing the soap froth off by piling the dishes together and turning the tap on them. "Perhaps, if I leave them piled up like this they'll dry themselves." She surveryed them hopefully.

"Better dry them, I suppose. Now for—"

The telephone bell rang shrilly.

"Suppose it's someone for Mum." Thomasina turned off the electricity under the egg she was boiling, and dawdled down the hall.

"Hello! Oh, it's you, Mum? You had your tram ticket, but forgot your purse? I'll just see if you left it in the bedroom. Mum, may I go to Napier with the bishop? I'll just catch him if I hurry. Am I crazy? No, it's just that—Yes, Mum, I'll see if your purse is on the dressing table. But may I—? Yes, right now, but may—? Yes, I'll be there in two ticks, but—Yes, I'll look before I say another word."

Thomasina sped along the hall to her mother's bedroom, picked up the purse off the dressing table and swooped back to the telephone.

"Yes, it's here, Mum. Yes, I have it right in my hand. Quite safe. Yes, on the dressing table. But, please, please, *please* may I go to Napier with the bishop and a friend of his, a clergyman? The strike's over, Mum. *Over.* Yes, the *Golden Star* will be sailing. Yes, he asked me. He did really. And Mrs. Sherwood asked me to stay before she left. And when you were out I didn't think I'd be able to go—It was *awful*."

"You're not *sure*? Oh, Mum, I've made the beds. *All* the beds, and washed the dishes. Yes, I scraped them first, and *rinsed* them. Yes, I boiled an egg for my lunch.

"Yes, I do know where he's staying. It's the Doncaster Hotel, and he's leaving just after lunch. Of course you could ring him. Yes, he's awf'lly old and awf'lly kind. He asked you to go, too, only I said you couldn't. And he doesn't think I'm a nuisance. Really he doesn't. You'll ring me back? Oh, Mum, thank you. *Thank you*, Mum."

With feet winged like Mercury's, Thomasina flew through the house. Her suitcase was packed in a matter of minutes. Her boiled egg was eaten in a matter of seconds.

So thorough was she that she had to unpack her tooth-brush to clean her teeth after lunch.

The telephone rang again.

"Yes, Mum, you're at Cousin Maud's? I knew the bishop wouldn't mind. And you put in a trunk call to Mrs. Sherwood, too. Oh, Mum, how did you know we'd be late? Yes, the bishop said we should. Mum, you said that to him? You told the bishop you hadn't intended to let me go, only you just couldn't refuse when you heard I'd done the beds and the dishes and my lunch? Oh, Mum, I'll be as good as gold, and you're a *darling*."

The front door bell was ringing.

Together Thomasina and the bishop walked to the gate.

"Mum let me go because I'd made the beds and washed the dishes. Oh, and made my own lunch. She said I was getting older and more responsible."

"Responsible?"

"That's it, sir. Remember you said perhaps it was all for the best that she was out when I came home, and I couldn't get permission to go? I probably wouldn't have done anything to help her, if she'd been there, then. I'd have been too busy pleading to be allowed to go."

Thomasina slowed her steps to the bishop's quiet pace.

"Yes," he said, with a smile creasing his wrinkled, rosy face, "things do tend to work out for the best—especially when you deserve them."

Thomasina blushed deep red with pleasure.

CHAPTER SEVENTEEN

RETURN TO THE MARDI GRAS

"I'LL GO first," Hongi whispered. He went through the hole with arms pushed forwards like a diver. The ragged edge of the opening seemed to close in as his body touched it, and for a breathless moment Lan wondered if Hongi could possibly wriggle through. But Hongi's body followed on to the stew-covered, squelchy ground.

Lan's ankle gave heavy beats of pain in time with his thumping heart. Now it was his turn. His hands sank into the stewy mud, and he heaved and pushed, and finally worked his way under the joists, until he could kneel and peer about him.

Hongi was waiting silently near the far corner of the shed where the piles were highest. Lan could hear his excited breathing, and sense his suppressed impatience.

Like a race horse all set to start, he thought, as he glanced angrily at his own ankle.

"If we go down hill through gardens until we get to a road, we'll keep out of sight of that house," Hongi whispered, with scarcely moving lips. Lan nodded agreement. He glanced at his watch, and silently turned it so that Hongi could see the hands indicating half past eight.

Cautiously the boys peered out. There was no one in sight, and the shed hid them from the house. Hongi gave a deep sigh. Suddenly a dog barked, and they froze, listening.

A single star glittered in the paling sky. Then, in a crouching position, Hongi glided over the rough grass. Not a twig broke, not a leaf rustled, not a branch stirred to betray his going. Crawling clumsily, dragging his throbbing ankle, Lan followed.

Bushes covered the hill thickly, and the smell of dry grass was soft on the warm air.

"It's almost too good to be true," Lan breathed deeply as he caught up with Hongi.

"We're not there yet, and we're dealing with desperate men." Hongi frowned, as he moved forward again, dodging from bush to bush.

A hedge dividing two gardens lay below them and they wriggled under a strand wire fence, and hurried silently in the shelter of the hedge.

"Mumme-ee-ee! Boys are in our garden!" a child's voice shrilled.

Lan froze, but Hongi, in front, gave a sudden dive, a twist and a wriggle, and disappeared from sight through a small cat hole at the bottom of the hedge. Lan followed him.

They could hear a woman's voice reassuring the child. "Come, we'll have a look. We'll see if there are any boys in the garden."

On the other side of the hedge, within two feet, the woman passed holding the child's hand.

"We'll look out the gate, and up the road," she said as they went by. A few minutes later, "There, you see, dear, no boys. Did they look like the lion you said was in the garden the other night?" Her voice was indulgent, that of a grown-up determined not to be hoodwinked by a child. They went towards the house again.

"But I did see two boys," the child's voice was insistent.

"Yes, dear," her mother agreed, polite in disbelief as the door closed.

Lan and Hongi glanced at the house on their side of the hedge. The blinds were down, and the windows were closed. The lawn was overgrown, and the hedge untrimmed. Silently the boys reached the gate. It creaked open when Lan pushed it, and of its own accord creaked shut, driven by a rusty spring.

For a moment the boys paused, watching, waiting, then slowly and deliberately, Lan limped down the sloping road, and Hongi kept in step. As they walked they tried to brush off the mixture of mud and soup that covered their arms, their hands and the front of their clothes.

Bending, Lan tore off some grass as they passed a clump growing by a fence post, and tried to wipe his shirt and his hands clean. The mud spread as he rubbed, and settled into the fibres of his cotton shirt. His hands looked smeared, and as muddy as ever.

Hongi shrugged at the futility of Lan's efforts.

They followed the road down, down, until they could see in the distance the lights on the giant Christmas trees on Marine Parade, and hear the raucous music of the Mardi Gras.

Lan's heart was thumping thickly. His ankle felt sudden arrows of pain. His breath came in short gasps, as if he had been running. "We'll soon be there," he muttered.

Hongi straightened his shoulders, and took a few deep

breaths before he answered. "I feel in goose flesh all over," he confessed. "Just knowing that at any minute, if we're not wary enough they may pounce."

Lan's voice was slow and determined, "They might kidnap other people, if they found out too much—"

He looked down and saw Hongi's clenched fist, and realised that Hongi's determination was as great as his own.

"There are telephone wires leading to this house," Lan paused. "We haven't any pennies to ring up from a 'phone box, so let's ask if we may ring up from here. I bet Uncle and Aunt and your mother are just about scared out of their wits, because we've disappeared. They'll have found out by now that we weren't at the police station."

"Too right," Hongi agreed. "I'll keep watch, if you ring them. I'd like to know if those smugglers have found out we've gone."

Lan rejoined Hongi in an incredibly short time.

"I got Uncle right away," he said rubbing more mud from his shirt. "I've never heard anyone so relieved to hear my voice. He'll ring your mother, and tell Aunt Jenny. I couldn't let him know all about it, because of the people in the house."

"But you told him enough?"

"Yes, he knows things are on the move. He's coming down to the Mardi Gras, but he's going to keep out of sight, and pretend that he doesn't know us, in case he gives the show away." Lan took a deep breath. He limped slowly, his lips tightening as spears of pain shot through his ankle.

They could smell the sea, and now the coloured lights

on the line of trees along Marine Parade twinkled in the deepening twilight.

The music from the Mardi Gras was loud on the air, raucous, insistent. Hongi slowed his steps to Lan's hesitant, limping pace. The thick coating of little pebbles under their feet were like trampled sugar, shifting and crunching. Their feet crushed drinking straws, empty cigarette packets, and a single ice-cream cone. Their ears were taut with listening, their eyes strained with wariness. Listening and watching. Listening and watching.

"Time?" Hongi breathed.

"Half past nine. They said ten o'clock."

Silently, as if by some secret agreement, they edged into the shadows beside the Pania stall, and crouched, waiting. They smelled the dust, the sweat, the cigarettes, the sweets, the oil and the engines that were part of the Mardi Gras. Their eyes were dazzled with the glittering lights, their ears numbed with the blaring, insistent music. And underlying it all were their throbbing heart beats, and the unspoken fear of trying to outwit determined and ruthless men.

In a world of whirling, gyrating amusement they waited silently. Minutes passed like hours. Lan's ankle ached with dull, angry throbbing.

Hongi inched Lan's wrist into position, so that he could see the hands of his watch. A shadow fell in front of the stall, and a man moved slowly. Uncle Bob. His eye skimmed over the shadows at the side of the stall as if he saw nothing. Deliberately he stood watching the merry-go-round, swinging faster and faster as if following the demanding, driving music.

Suddenly, before they expected it, as if hiding under the

umbrella of harsh sound, came a few rhythmic notes. Lan and Hongi stiffened, eyes gleaming coldly, ears straining.

The compelling notes of "The Roundabout". Breathlessly they moved to the corner of the stall. The thin man, who had trapped them in the shed, pocketed a parcel handed to him by the stall-keeper. He turned away quickly.

As he moved, Lan's swollen ankle shot out, causing him to stumble. Hongi, with a flying football tackle, crashed him to the ground. Before the man had time to move Lan was sitting firmly on his chest, pinioning his arms above his head.

Two Pania statuettes fell, dully thudding into the gravel at Hongi's feet. As he looked up, the stall-keeper vaulted nimbly over the other statuettes, dropped lightly on to the pebbles, and, with a sudden twist slid between the stall and the gathering onlookers, and broke away into the darkness.

With one fluid movement Hongi was after him. A policeman, young and serious, appeared through the watching crowd like the genie out of the lamp. Earnestly, deliberately, he took out his notebook and turned to Lan. "What's the matter, son?" His pencil poised for the kill like a harpoon.

"Diamonds," Lan explained, breathlessly. "Smuggled diamonds."

"Diamonds?" The notebook wavered. "I've been on the look-out for them. Not a sign of anything. Just you be sure you're right, young fellow."

"It's true." Lan did not relax his hold on the man whose arms he held pinioned. "They're in his coat pocket, this one. They whistle "The Roundabout" as a sort of password."

"They've whistled it already? Didn't hear it myself. Sergeant told me to listen for it. Didn't like to tell him then that I can't recognise tunes. I'm tone deaf. Anyhow, let's have a look. Let him up."

"I've just got one of the Pania statuettes in that pocket," the man twisted round, as Lan loosened his hold "Got it for my little girl. I promised it to her for her birthday."

"You could prove it," Lan said, softly. He released the man's right hand, and indicated the pocket of his coat.

"There you are! It's a statuette, just like I said. I'll charge you with assault and battery for this," he snarled. "And aren't you the boy—?" He gazed in amazement at Lan.

The constable took the statuette.

"Yes, it's as he said." He opened up his notebook again, and poised his pencil. "It's certainly a clear case of assault and battery. Children's court, of course."

"There's a hinge on the side, and it opens up," Lan rasped.

There was a sudden movement through the crowd. Uncle Bob and Hongi, followed by two burly policemen, stood looking down at Lan and the man on the ground.

"Diamonds!" the young constable was peering inside the statuette. "I've never seen so many at the same time."

"Hm-m!" A police sergeant cleared his throat disapprovingly. "We'll take all statements at the station."

"Any luck, Hongi?" Lan asked, quietly.

"No, that stall-holder was too quick for me. He just seemed to melt away in the darkness."

"And now," the police sergeant said, as they left the police station half an hour later, "now for the *Golden Star*. It might be useful if you all came." he turned to Uncle, Bob, Hongi and Lan. "Surprise tactics, you know."

CHAPTER EIGHTEEN

THE REWARD

THE POLICE CAR sped through the night. Heavy clouds piled up over the watery moon as two policemen with Uncle Bob, Hongi and Lan raced towards the *Golden Star*.

"There!" Hongi cried, suddenly. "I'm sure that's the stall-keeper. He's seen us! He's running!"

The car leapt forward. Then, with a cough and a sigh it spluttered, ran slower, and slower, and finally rolled to a halt.

"It's the petrol lead!" the sergeant growled. "It'd just have to happen again when we were getting into the thick of things. We'll never get it going in time." He shook the car, rocking and pushing it in a vain attempt to unblock the pipe. "We haven't a radio telephone in this car, either. It's one we use for emergencies. Emergencies!" He gave a hollow laugh.

The light of an approaching car spotlighted the little group gazing at the police car, resting gently and obstinately in the middle of the road.

Hongi listened with a widening grin. "Well, jumping cricket bats!" he beamed. "We couldn't have asked for anything better." He waved in wild excitement. The car, looking like a cartoon of a vintage tourer, flapped its tattered sidescreens to a gliding halt.

"Oh, no!" the sergeant groaned. "Not that. Think of my dignity. Just imagine how Napier would burst its sides at the sight of the police flapping along in an old rattle-trap, chasing a suspect at about three miles an hour. Boys like their little jokes, I know, but you've gone a bit too far this time."

Hongi did not seem to hear. He was talking urgently to the young man in the car.

"Gosh!" Lan turned to Uncle Bob. "Hongi and I saw this car before, and without looking, Hongi said it was a Bentley. He didn't even laugh when he saw what it looked like."

"Well, jump in." The driver, a young man with laughing eyes, opened the doors. "I'm Tony Derwent," he added. The constable and the sergeant sheepishly eased their bulk into the back seat. Lan followed, while Uncle Bob and Hongi crowded into the front with the young man.

The car shot forward with the unerring grace of an arrow from a bow. One of the sidescreens descended in a flying arc to the roadway. The policemen clutched the back of the front seat, and stared in astonishment at a Jaguar, as they streaked past it. The open-mouthed occupants of the Jaguar, peering from its windows, looked as if at an apparition.

"What—what sort of engine has it?" Lan stammered in his excitement.

"It's a Bentley chassis. Dad gave it to me last year. He got a hefty wool cheque, and gave me this, as a share in it. Its own body had been smashed in an accident, and I put on this old vintage top." Tony swooped round a heavy truck.

Hongi beamed at the dazed truck driver as they passed. "We sure get plenty of fun with the old rattle-trap.

We ease along at about five miles an hour until we see one of those snooty stream-lined jobs, and then, whoops, before you can say 'apple pie!' we're smoothing along in front. I always give them a slight bow and a smile as we pass," Tony Derwent chuckled.

"There!" Hongi peered into the darkness. "I'm sure I saw the stall-keeper. He'll never suspect we're in this car. See, he's not even hurrying."

As he spoke the man turned furtively, saw the speeding car, and took to his heels. The vintage car slowed to five miles an hour and gained slowly on the fugitive.

"That'll reassure him," Uncle Bob leaned forward, peering into the darkness. "Yes, he's slowing down. Where is he? I can't see him now."

"Neither can I," Lan strained forwards.

They passed several parked cars, but the man seemed to have melted into thin air.

As they passed a corner a car behind them throbbed to life, turned, and roared away into the darkness.

"There's our man," the sergeant gritted in anger.

The Bentley described a wide circle as it turned, and speared into the darkness. The remaining side window sailed into the night. The wind whistled through the openings. Something unseen fell with a metallic clang on to the road.

"We're all shook up," the younger policeman ventured a remark.

In the distance, heading towards Bluff Hill, they could see the other car, and could hear its roaring whine as it bounded towards the hill road. The Bentley lunged in pursuit.

"I can't put her flat out, or she'd shake off the old rattle-trap on top." Tony stared at the road, winding darkly upwards.

"Just as well," the sergeant grunted. "You'd probably shake us off, too."

The Bentley slowed imperceptibly. The whine of the car in front came thin and clear on the still night air. Suddenly Lan grasped Hongi's shoulder. "He might be making for the house where they locked us in the shed. I've recognised some of the trees we passed on the way down."

"Locked you in a shed?" the sergeant asked quickly.

Breathlessly they explained about their capture, and their escape from the shed.

"An old red house? With a shed behind it in the garden?" the constable asked eagerly. "I know that place. Mind, it's only a hunch, but I've been a bit suspicious about it before. If you turn here," he said quietly to Tony Derwent, "we'll cut him off before he gets near the house."

"Always supposing that we haven't been thrown off the trail already," the sergeant said, gloomily.

The road snaked upwards in the darkness. The car headlamps turned the street into a ribbon of light. With screaming tyres they skidded round a hill corner. There was a pungent smell of burnt rubber.

"Hrm!" the sergeant cleared his throat disapprovingly.

The road narrowed, and again twisted upwards.

"He's got to pass here," the constable said, as if to himself. "If you parked your car across the road, a hundred yards or so away from one of these bends, the stall-keeper wouldn't see it in time to turn back quickly, but he'd see it before he ran into it."

"Then," Hongi interrupted, excitedly, "he'd get out to try to shift the Bentley, or he'd slow down to turn, and we could be hiding, and pounce on him."

"Pounce," the sergeant grunted, shifting his bulk as the car slowed into the proposed position, "pounce is not the word I'd have used. You have, however, the general idea." He turned to the constable. "Later we'll get those fellows who kidnapped the boys down to the station for questioning. They sound like pretty tough customers to me."

"You've got one of them," Lan reminded him.

"S-sh!" Hongi whispered, urgently. "I can hear that car coming."

They melted into the cover of the bushes on the edge of the road—Uncle Bob, the young constable and Lan, still limping painfully, on one side, with the sergeant, Hongi and Tony Derwent on the other.

A car swiftly rounded the bend and pulled up with a scream of brakes. Silently it was surrounded.

"Why, Constable, or should I say Sergeant?" a honey-laden voice purred. "You did startle me." A pair of wide, kitten-like eyes gazed in wonderment, and the driver shook back her blonde hair, wafting a breath of perfume on the still night air.

"Oh, excuse me, miss, we were looking for a man— I suppose you didn't see anyone?"

"No. Oh, let me see! There was a man on a bicycle, only he didn't come up the hill. No, how silly of me! That was yesterday! Good night, Inspector, so sorry I can't help you."

The car indicator flipped into position to show an intended right-hand turn, and at the same moment the back door of the car was flung open, and Hongi, with a muffled shout, jerked a rug from a mound on the floor. The sergeant, peering into the car, found his eyes rivetted to the furtive and startled gaze of the stall-keeper.

"Why it's the young feller-me-lad that saved me life!" a familiar voice greeted them, as the policemen, Uncle Bob, Hongi and Lan climbed the gangway to the *Golden Star*, and Mr. Puddick detached himself from the rail, and beamed upon them. When he saw the policemen his smile faded.

"Now, don't tell me that Bulke reported you for taking that watch." He spat neatly to leeward. "Anyhow, it wasn't a full watch, as you might say. Just a case for a watch," he said earnestly to the sergeant.

"You see, it was like this. The captain gave it to Mr. Bulke to leave at a jeweller's to get mended, and I went with him. Well, that jeweller did a funny thing. He went into a back room, took out the works for mending, and gave us back the case to give the captain. I've never seen a jeweller give back the case before. And neither had Mr. Bulke. But he put it in his cabin till the captain came back, and it just disappeared—hasn't been found yet."

"Hm-m!" the sergeant cleared his throat. "You were with Mr. Bulke from the time the captain handed him the watch until it was given to the jeweller?"

"That's right, Sergeant."

"And Mr. Bulke didn't look inside it? He didn't examine the works, for instance?"

"No. Why should he, Sergeant? Anyhow, the captain said that the spring for opening it was faulty, and he was very particular that we shouldn't touch it. 'Just hand it into the jeweller's' he said, and gave us the name and address."

"Hm-m!" The sergeant's constriction in the throat seemed to be becoming chronic.

"And there's another little matter about signalling," the sergeant took out his notebook.

"Signalling? Oh, perhaps you mean that signalling lamp in the blue car the captain's friend lent Mr. Bulke? We don't know anything about it either. He's the purser, and signalling isn't much in his line. The signalling lamp belongs to the owner of the car."

"And Mr. Bulke has his address?"

"Sure thing, Sergeant, and the jeweller's address, too."

"We'll haul him in as well," the young constable said, eagerly.

"Perhaps," Lan looked thoughtful, and his finger-tips tapped together, "they used Mr. Bulke as a cover—a sort of stooge."

"In that case, I'd be very interested to see the captain," the sergeant straightened his back.

"And then," Lan said to Aunt Jenny later, "we all —"

There was a thunderous knock on the front door.

"Who on earth, at this time of night?" Lan paused.

"It is, undoubtedly, Thomasina and the bishop. He's staying here to-night, and we've invited Thomasina to stay for the rest of the holidays." Uncle Bob stood up.

"It won't be a rest, whatever else it is," Hongi grinned, as Uncle Bob opened the door, and Thomasina and the bishop, triumphant and weary, sank on to the nearest chairs.

"They've got the smugglers safe and sound at the police station," Aunt Jenny said quietly.

"I knew I'd be too late," Thomasina groaned, "but I'll send all my photos along as evidence in the morning." She stretched her legs straight out in front of her, as if smoothing out imaginary kinks in them.

"I hope," the bishop said mildly, "that I'm not showing undue curiosity, but would someone please tell me what happened?"

"Lan found an empty watch case in Mr. Bulke's cabin, and it had scratches all over it inside—" Hongi began.

"The cabin? What a pity!" The bishop showed suitable concern.

"No, sir, the watch case. And then Hongi and I were kidnapped again. They were going to drown us," Lan paused, and went on quietly, "we managed to escape, and caught up with two of the men at the Pania stall at the Mardi Gras. That "Roundabout" song gave the show away. They whistle that as a sort of password before they collect the diamonds in hollowed-out Pania statuettes."

The bishop was silent. His hands gripped the arms of his chair. He leaned forward.

"The police brought us to identify and to confront some of the suspects, up on Bluff Hill and on the *Golden Star*," Hongi explained.

"Oh, yes," Lan said, "we all went to Mr. Bulke's cabin, and told him where to find the watch case. And do you know, it was there just where I'd pushed it, behind the box!"

Aunt Jenny's eyes gleamed. "Shows what sort of house-keepers they are on that ship. Any woman would have swept it out days ago!"

Uncle Bob gave a shout of laughter.

"When they'd taken the captain to the police station, we all went off to find the owner of the blue car—the constable seemed to think we'd be able to identify him. And what do you know! He was the burly one who had helped to kidnap us. He'd just found out we weren't in the shed!" Hongi guffawed loudly. "I don't think I'll ever forget the look on his face as he opened the door when the constable rang, and there we were, smiling at him on the door mat!"

Aunt Jenny shuddered. "I can't forget that they kidnapped you both, and were going to drown you—"

"Well, they can't do anything like that, now," Uncle Bob reassured her. "They admitted everything when they found we knew they had been using the watch and the Panias to smuggle out the diamonds in small amounts, in case they got caught."

"Where did they hide the diamonds on the ship?" the bishop asked.

"In the hollow chromium leg of a table. They took me in completely about Mr. Bulke, too. Shrewd, framing him like that. But they didn't get away with it. Mr. Bulke is just what he seems, a well-meaning, jolly sort of man, zealous in guarding the good name of his ship, human enough to like throwing sticks for Wuffit, and mighty useful for getting us out of jams."

"Well," the bishop said, folding his hands over his stomach, "I'm sure I don't know what my sister will say when I tell her about my holiday."

"Perhaps, sir, she'll want to come, too, next time," Uncle Bob laughed. He turned to Lan and Hongi. "I'm proud of you both, and of Thomasina, too. You've been a credit to your father's training, Lan." The boy beamed his delight.

Uncle Bob's pipe seemed to be drawing to his satisfaction. "By the way, there was a reward offered in England for information leading to the arrest of the smugglers." Uncle Bob turned to the bishop. "The police sergeant says that Hongi and Lan will share it—£250 each."

"Thomasina, too!" Hongi and Lan said, as if in one breath.

"Gosh!" said Thomasina, and she became quite pink right up to the roots of her red hair.

"And there's the bishop, he saved us, too," Lan added.

"And Mr. Bulke. What would we have done without Mr. Bulke?" Hongi asked.

"I demand my share," the bishop's eyes twinkled. "My pound of flesh, I'm sure you'll call it. I want," he said slowly, "a clear and well-written account of your adventures. What do you say, Thomasina, Hongi and Lan?"

"Done!" they shouted.

"It will," the bishop smiled gently, "add greatly to the interest of my library. And, of course," he added, "to my education."

"As for Mr. Bulke," Uncle Bob pressed down the tobacco in his pipe, "we've invited him to stay with us. There'll be another delay in the sailing of the *Golden Star*. It looks as if they'll have to replace the captain."

"What will you do with your share, Hongi?" Lan asked.

Hongi stood rubbing his left ankle with his right foot as he thought. "Well, I'd like to buy presents for Mom, and for Uncle Bob and Aunt Jenny. Oh, and Wuffit, eh?"

"May I make a contribution?" the bishop seemed to have been dozing quietly, but now he opened his eyes. "I have a somewhat elderly typewriter, which I was going to replace. I should be very pleased if you would all accept it for the Junior C.I.B. to use for writing about their adventures. That is, of course, when you are not using invisible ink. Would you like it?"

"Would we like it?" Hongi, Thomasina and Lan breathed delightedly. "Just you wait until you read our story, sir!"

"What'll you get for yourself, Thomasina?" Aunt Jenny asked.

"Well, I'll buy a new pair of shorts before Mum sees the hole I tore in my others this morning. Oh, and a new bathing suit. I don't know yet what else. What about you, Lan?"

"I'm going to put most of it away after I've bought a few presents. Funny thing is, that though I used to hate school, I've got quite interested in it lately."

"Don't tell me that later on you want to go to the university?" Hongi seemed deeply shocked.

"Well, yes, I do."

"Why, blow me down with a feather," Hongi drawled, "that's what I want to do, too!"

"Oh," Thomasina laughed suddenly, "it won't be for years, but I guess I'll have to go right along, too. Can't let you two have all the adventures."

"We'll be having lots of adventures before then," Lan assured her.

"You could," Uncle Bob said, as the clock struck twelve, "be right."